**"Today you did something
I have been wanting to do
for the past year. You avenged me."**

Before Longarm could pull away, Jill flung both arms around his neck and fastened her lips to his. He found it impossible not to respond in kind as she propelled him backward toward the bed. The back of his knees struck the edge of the mattress, and he fell suddenly back, Jill Dunstrom still clinging to him.

"Ma'am...!" he muttered, pulling his lips free of hers and attempting to unwind her arms from around his neck. "There's no need for you to thank me for what I did...!"

"Don't call me ma'am! You make me sound like a schoolteacher! And I *am* going to thank you for what you did!"

TABOR EVANS

LONGARM

AND THE JAMES COUNTY WAR

A JOVE BOOK

LONGARM AND THE JAMES COUNTY WAR

A Jove Book/published by arrangement with
the author

PRINTING HISTORY
Jove edition/March 1984

ISBN: 0-515-06264-2

Jove books are published by The Berkley Publishing Group,
200 Madison Avenue, New York, N.Y. 10016. The words
"A JOVE BOOK" and the "J" with sunburst are trademarks
belonging to Jove Publications, Inc.

PRINTED IN THE UNITED STATES OF AMERICA

LONGARM

AND THE
JAMES COUNTY WAR

Chapter 1

It was a bright morning and Denver City's high, clear air was not yet fogged with coal smoke, soot, and the finely trampled essence of horse manure. Once again Longarm was hurrying up Colfax in a futile attempt to put behind him that strange, clinging, haunting smell of burning leaves.

A big man, lean and muscular, with the body of a young athlete, he moved with a swift, catlike stride. His seamed and sun-burnished face spoke eloquently of long rides in the face of raw, unforgiving winds. His eyes were a gunmetal blue; his close-cropped hair was the color of aged tobacco leaf. Adding much to the single-minded ferocity now stamped on his features was his well trimmed, drooping longhorn mustache. Better than

1

six feet tall, he loomed above most of the men and women passing him, a hurrying, preoccupied giant of a man who hardly noticed how swiftly those in his path ducked aside.

Longarm's preoccupation stemmed from the fact that it was employment he was after—and soon. For too long he had tarried in this sinful, mile-high Sodom and Gomorrah, and he was determined that this day Billy Vail would dig up some excuse to rescue him from Denver's gaudy fleshpots before he succumbed to its lotus-like, enervating embrace entirely. Not that there was anything wrong with the lovely young widow who had comforted him the night before, but she sure as hell was enervating. He knew damn well that if he spent many more such nights in this town, he would grow to like it so well that he would end up as soft as tallow and as miserable as a caged cougar.

Glancing at his pocket watch as he passed the U. S. Mint at Cherokee and Colfax, he turned the corner and headed for the federal building. Once inside, he strode through the swarm of officious lawyers and politicians crowding the downstairs lobby, hurried upstairs, and pushed his way through a door that bore the gilt-lettered legend: UNITED STATES MARSHAL, FIRST DISTRICT COURT OF COLORADO.

In the outer office Henry, the pink-cheeked clerk, was playing upon his typewriter, the newfangled piece of machinery clacking at an infernal pitch as Longarm swept on past him.

"Mr. Long!" the clerk cried, looking up. "Marshal Vail wants you to go right in!"

"That's just what I was planning to do, old son," he

2

told the clerk as he knocked once on Billy Vail's door and went on in.

Vail glanced up from his cluttered desk. "On time for once, Longarm? You must be getting restless."

Longarm closed the door behind him and slumped into the red morocco leather armchair beside Vail's desk. "That's right, Billy. I'm about ready for far places."

Vail glanced up at him and grunted. "You do have that look in your eye, now that you mention it. Something between a caged grizzly and a wet hen."

Longarm looked hopefully at the marshal. "You got something for me?"

Billy Vail nodded cagily.

"What is it?" Longarm went on.

"Something . . . unusual, Longarm. I wouldn't be suggesting it if I didn't know how restless you was to shake this place—and I wasn't so anxious myself to nail this son of a bitch."

"You got someone you want me to bring in?"

"That's it," said Vail.

"Sounds simple enough."

"It ain't. Not by a damn sight."

"Maybe you better explain that."

Vail sighed and brushed his hand down over his round, pale face. For a man who had once been as rangy as a wild Longhorn bull, Longarm mused, it must be pure hell to have to carry around that lard. Longarm did not envy the U. S. marshal his desk job—not one bit.

"This here fellow I'm sending you after," Vail said, pausing for effect, "is the sheriff of Harmony, Montana."

Longarm stirred thoughtfully in his chair and took a

3

cheroot from his pocket. "Guess you're right at that. This won't be so simple. Go on, Billy."

"The name he's going by now is Tex Bingham. When I knew him, years ago, it was Bonham—Bart Bonham."

"Maybe we better eat this here apple one bite at a time, Billy. What's he wanted for?"

"He killed a nephew of mine, Charlie Vail. Charlie was more than a nephew to me, Longarm. He was the son I never had. I taught him how to bait his first fish-hook, and how to send a tin can along the ground firing from the waist. Maybe I spent too much time showing him how to use a gun and not enough time telling him when to use it."

"He went bad?" Longarm asked.

"Soon as I rode out, Bart and he started robbing stages. They weren't too bright about it and they got caught. They were sent to Yuma, but broke free. Ten miles from Yuma, I found Charlie dead, shot once from close range. Bart's horse was nearby. It had gone lame. The way I figure it, Bart shot Charlie for his horse."

Longarm puffed for a moment on his cheroot, then closed one eye and peered thoughtfully at Vail. "Billy, you didn't have anything to do with that breakout from Yuma, did you?"

Billy Vail shrugged. "I ain't sayin' yes and I ain't sayin' no. But one thing I will say—it was before I joined the law."

Longarm grinned sardonically. "Which is why you knew which horse was Charlie's and which one was Bart's."

"I want Bart, Longarm. And all I can give you is a

4

bench warrant that's years old. It might not even be legal. But I want this son of a bitch."

"You sure this here Tex Bingham is Bonham?" Longarm asked.

"Sure enough, but I could be wrong."

"Then you'll want me to make damn sure before I haul the fellow in."

"That's right."

"How'd you get a line on him?"

Billy Vail smiled crookedly. "He sent Washington a letter. Seems he figures there's a range war brewing in his county and he wants some help. The thing is, Washington sent his letter along, and I recognized the handwriting."

"You want to explain that?"

"When I gave Charlie and him them two horses outside Yuma, I gave them both a bill of sale for the horses, and had each of them sign a receipt. I never forgot the way Bart scrawled his signature, and it just jumped out at me when I saw the way this Bingham signed that letter he wrote to Washington. All the letters, especially the b's, the h's, and the m's, were the same—and the backward way he scrawled them. I dug up those two receipts and compared his signature with the one on the letter."

"Let me see."

Vail took a wrinkled, yellowed slip of paper out of a side drawer and, smoothing it carefully, placed it down beside the letter from the sheriff of Harmony, Montana. One glance at the handwriting of both and Longarm nodded, convinced.

"Crazy," he mused, sitting back in his chair and glancing up at Vail. "Him sending that letter, not dreaming it would turn up on the desk of the lawman whose nephew he shot."

"It's a small world," Vail said coldly, a note of mean triumph in his voice. "All it takes is patience. On your way down, sooner or later you meet all them sons of bitches you passed on your way up."

"There's just one thing, Billy."

"What's that?"

"If this jasper is Bonham, he knows you helped him and Charlie escape from Yuma. Seems to me he wouldn't keep quiet about a thing like that. You'd lose your job."

"You think I care about that now? Look at me. I'm turning to suet behind this blamed desk."

"And you might go to jail."

Vail shook his head. "No danger of that for either of us. I'll get probation and this here Bonham will likely get a pardon. All he'll have to do is prove he's been leading an exemplary life since his escape. Hell, he's a lawman now. We take care of our own."

Longarm frowned. "Then I don't understand what you want. If bringing him in won't get him anything more than a slap on the wrist, why bother?"

"He killed Charlie. I don't just want him brought in, Longarm. I want him to pay for what he did. The way Charlie paid."

Longarm almost choked on the cheroot. He didn't think he was hearing right. "You want to spell that out for me again, Billy?"

"Relax, Longarm. I don't want you to kill him."

"Then what?"

"Just bring him in," Vail said coldly.

Longarm puffed for a long moment on his cheroot. "I see. And you'll take care of the rest."

Marshal Billy Vail did not reply. It was not necessary.

Longarm was in a quandary. He did not want to be a party to bringing down Billy Vail. But if he brought in Bonham, and Billy was so foolish as to vent his rage on the man, that was precisely what would result. And that would make for a sorry end to Billy Vail's long and honorable career as a law officer.

Vail read the hesitation in Longarm's face. "If you won't go, I'll send Wallace."

"I'll blow the whistle on you, Billy," said Longarm.

Vail smiled thinly. "No, you won't."

Longarm sighed. Vail was right about that. He knew that Longarm would never do such a thing. The two men had grown pretty close over the years. All Longarm could do now was try to prevent Billy Vail from acting un-wisely.

"I'll go after this here sheriff," Longarm said. "But I should warn you, Billy. When I bring him back, I will not let you touch him. For your own good *and* mine."

"Just bring him back."

Longarm stubbed his cheroot out in the ashtray on the corner of Vail's desk, then tossed the butt into the cuspidor. "Get the tickets and travel vouchers ready while I collect my gear."

Vail rose and nodded. "I'll have everything ready for you when you get back. The first train heading north leaves at three this afternoon."

Without another word, Longarm left Vail's office. As

7

he passed the clerk, he did not even bother to pester Henry. He was too preoccupied. For the first time in Longarm's life, he hoped the man he was being sent to bring in would be gone when he got there.

At Hammer Fork, Montana, Longarm left the train and took a stage for Harmony. He had just enough time to fortify himself for the ride with a shot of rye purchased at a saloon across from the depot before the stage pulled up in front of the express office. Deciding to keep his carpetbag with him, he moved past the jehu who was stowing baggage and gear in the rear boot and climbed aboard.

The stage had three other passengers. Beside him sat a beefy city dude, with a ruddy face, who appeared to be a drummer. A gaunt, weather-beaten old timer was sitting in the corner across from him; he had the neat, threadbare look of a struggling rancher. Directly across from Longarm sat a very beautiful young woman, auburn-haired, with amber-flecked brown eyes and a dusky complexion. She was wearing a dark green traveling outfit that looked costly enough to make her a rich man's wife or daughter.

The jehu poked his head in the window. "Get set. We'll be rolling directly," he said.

Longarm poked his head out of the window and watched as the driver tied down the boot's apron, then swung up into the box. As he did so, the shotgun messenger, carrying a Winchester instead of a shotgun, came out of the express office and clambered quickly up beside the driver.

With a wild yell and a pistol-shot crack of the whip, the six-horse team was turned loose. The Concord coach gave a great lurch, swayed wildly on its thoroughbraces, and shot forward. The adobe buildings and frame houses of Hammer Fork swept past, then disappeared behind the rumbling coach. The jehu kept his team running hard for a spell, causing the dust to roil up from under the pounding hoofs and spinning wheels.

Pulling his head back inside, Longarm rested it against the plush cushion. The sun laid its heavy hand on the coach and soon the interior became as stuffy as Longarm had anticipated it would, though it was not as bad as the train coach he had quit not so long before.

Longarm pushed his hat back off his forehead and loosened his string tie. The drummer fanned himself with his narrow-brimmed hat while his pudgy face got redder and redder. The old cattleman dozed, his bony chin resting on his chest, seemingly unmindful of the heat, the dust, or the bumpy, swaying motion of the stage. The woman in the green dress removed first her gloves, then her saucy little hat. Finally she took an embroidered handkerchief from her sleeve and patted her forehead with it, smiling faintly at Longarm as she did so.

He met her gaze and smiled back. The woman seemed to be acknowledging that Longarm's neat and somewhat striking appearance made him a gentleman in her eyes. Longarm was not surprised. As usual, despite the long, fatiguing train ride, he was dressed well, in keeping with the rigid department regulations concerning the appearance of federal marshals.

He was wearing a snuff-brown Stetson, which until

9

a moment before he had kept positioned carefully on his head, dead center and tilted slightly forward, cavalry style. The hat's crown was telescoped in the Colorado rider's fashion, a legacy from his youth when he'd run away to ride in the War. His neat, well-tailored tweed suit and vest were brown. His shirt was blue-gray, with a black shoestring tie knotted at the neck. His boots, fashioned of cordovan leather, were low-heeled army issue. They were a compromise. A federal marshal spent as much time afoot as he did in the saddle, and Longarm found that he could run with surprising speed for a man his size in his snug, tight-fitting boots.

As Longarm returned the woman's smile, he did not fail to notice the wedding band that graced her hand. It was of truly prodigious proportions. As Longarm could well understand, the fellow who had roped her wanted the world to know she was out of circulation.

"Going far, ma'am?" he asked.

"As far as Harmony. And you?" she inquired.

"I'm heading for the same place," Longarm told her.

"Are you planning on settling there?"

"No, ma'am. I just have some business to transact in your fair community."

She sighed. "You refer to Harmony as a fair community. I only wish it were so, Mr. . . . ?"

"Long, ma'am—Custis Long."

"And I am Jill Dunstrom."

He nodded. "Pleased to meet you, ma'am."

She seemed intent on continuing the conversation, and was undoubtedly about to inquire into the nature of the business he had to transact in Harmony, but Longarm directed his glance out the window of the stage and frowned in concentration. Jill Dunstrom immediately caught herself and leaned back in her seat, her pretty lips pursing.

She knew when a man preferred his own thoughts to the somewhat inconsequential prattle of a woman, and she seemed perfectly willing to accept Longarm's dismissal. Longarm was more than a little intrigued by Jill Dunstrom, but since he intended at least to begin this mission under cover, he felt he had no other way to forestall the woman's polite but probing inquiries except by discouraging any further conversation.

As soon as he arrived in Harmony, Longarm planned to seek out Sheriff Tex Bingham and tell him he had been sent by the Denver federal marshal in answer to his letter. But, as he would explain to the lawman, until Longarm got his bearings, he wanted no one else to know the reason for his presence in Harmony. That the sheriff was himself a target of Longarm's investigation would of course never be revealed until Longarm could be absolutely certain that Sheriff Bingham was indeed the same Bart Bonham who had murdered Billy Vail's nephew.

Just what Longarm would do when that time came he preferred not to dwell on for now.

The stage made a scheduled stop at the Pine Creek stage station for a change of horses. A couple of miles farther on it made another, unscheduled stop. They were traveling through rough country, all brush and rocks, and the jehu was taking it easy up a long grade when a rifle shot cracked. With a shuddering creak of leather and the

11

jingle of harness, the driver pulled up hastily.

"What is it? What's happened?" Jill Dunstrom cried.

The drummer sat up, scared. "A holdup for sure!" he muttered.

The old cattleman woke up, but said not a word. He did not even look concerned.

Longarm stuck his head out the side window and saw that the team's off leader was down, dead in its tracks. Three riders were emerging from a jumble of huge rocks just ahead of them. They wore their bandannas over the lower portions of their faces and kept their weapons trained on the jehu and the shotgun messenger as they swiftly dismounted.

The jehu was cursing bitterly, but the shotgun messenger was conspicuous by his silence.

"We ain't carrying no strongbox, you sons of bitches," the driver snapped.

"That don't make no never mind," one of the road agents said. "If you ain't carrying any express, we'll just have to take up a collection." The man turned his attention to the coach. "Everybody out!" he cried. "Pronto! Line up along the stage!"

Longarm pushed open the door and stepped down, the others following hastily out after him. Though Longarm was wearing his Colt in his cross-draw rig and was itching to go for it, he was reluctant to try anything for fear of drawing fire that would injure the other passengers, Mrs. Jill Dunstrom in particular.

The youngest of the road agents frisked Longarm quickly, found his .44, and tossed it into the brush. Before he stepped back, he glimpsed Longarm's watch chain and snatched at it. When he did, he pulled forth both the watch and the .44-caliber derringer attached to it as a watch fob. Astonished, he showed his companions what he had found, then pocketed both the watch and Longarm's derringer.

"Search the others," said the leader of the road agents. "We don't want no more surprises."

No one else was armed, and on the road agent's orders each man—including the jehu and the shotgun messenger—opened his wallet and dropped what greenbacks and coins he possessed into the battered black Stetson held out before them.

The road agent who took the collection was a small, wiry Mexican, judging from his dusky skin, brown eyes, and black hair. He seemed somewhat shy when he held the Stetson out in front of Jill Dunstrom, but when she dropped a fat wad of greenbacks into his hat, his eyes became happy slits as he fished it out and tossed it to the leader.

Obviously pleased, the fellow snatched the wad out of the air and pocketed it swiftly. A huge bear of a fellow, he seemed to be in easy control of the situation. The youngest of the three, however, seemed edgy and quite ill at ease. Longarm did not like the careless way he waved his huge Colt about, his finger on the trigger, the hammer cocked.

Glancing at the big road agent, Longarm said, "Tell your young friend there to point that gun elsewhere or put it away. It might go off any second, and it could be the lady he hits."

The big fellow strode up to Longarm and clubbed him on the side of the head with his revolver. As the back of Longarm's skull slammed into the side of the coach, he felt his knees buckle slightly. He would have slipped to the ground had not the old cattleman reached over quickly and held him up. Shaking his head to clear it, Longarm steadied himself by leaning back against the stage, then pushed himself away from it.

"That wasn't at all necessary," Jill Dunstrom snapped at the road agent. "What are you, some kind of animal?"

"That's right, Mrs. Dunstrom. And a hungry animal at that."

As he spoke, he stuck his sixgun into his belt, took her wrist in one hand, and with the other pulled off her oversized wedding band.

"Damn you!" she cried.

"Leave it, why don't you," spoke up the cattleman, his grizzled face hard, his eyes gleaming like anthracite. "It has meaning for her and wouldn't be worth much to you."

"Shut up!" snarled the road agent, backing up and taking his sixgun from his belt. Brandishing the weapon menacingly, he cried, "Turn around and start walking! All of you!"

Jill turned and started to walk. The drummer joined her, the cattleman, the jehu, and the shotgun messenger following close on their heels. Longarm lagged slightly behind. Reaching the rear of the stage, he glanced back. The road agents were intent on mounting up.

Swiftly, he ducked around the stage's rear boot and continued around the stage. Doubling back, he came out on the other side of the horses, jumped over the dead horse, and came out alongside the nearest of the road agents—the young, nervous one. Reaching up, he snatched the youngster's left hand and dragged him from

14

the saddle. The young man was going for his sixgun even as he slammed into the ground. Rolling over, he managed to get off a shot at Longarm.

The round missed and Longarm flung himself onto him, wrested the revolver from his grasp, and brought the barrel around with all the force he could muster, catching him on the side of the head. As the young agent went limp, Longarm aimed the sixgun at the Mexican. The astonished highwayman had pulled up his horse and was now staring down at Longarm in some consternation. Foolishly, he went for his gun. Longarm fired. The Mexican cried out and grabbed at his shoulder. He almost toppled from his horse, but managed somehow to keep himself in the saddle, pull his horse around, and gallop off.

But the other road agent had no such intention. He had already wheeled his horse and was now galloping straight for Longarm.

"That's my brother!" the man cried, his bandanna slipping down now to reveal his lean, shocked face. "Leave him be!"

He leveled his sixgun at Longarm and fired. The round whispered ominously past Longarm's cheek. Longarm aimed carefully at the oncoming rider's broad shirtfront and squeezed the trigger. The round opened a neat hole in his shirt and the force of the slug slammed the highwayman backward. The horse kept coming as the big fellow tumbled off. Longarm ducked just in time, the horse's hooves clearing his head only by inches.

As quickly as that it was all over.

Turning his attention to the younger highwayman, Longarm found to his dismay that the crack to the man's skull had been fatal. He had not intended it to be so, but in his haste, there had been no way for him to temper the savagery of the blow. Pulling off the bandanna, he found himself looking at a youngster no older than seventeen or eighteen. The kid was too young to die, perhaps, but dead he was, and he had his older brother as well as Longarm to thank for that.

With Longarm helping them, the jehu and the shotgun messenger wrapped the two dead highwaymen in their slickers and dumped them into the coach's rear boot. Meanwhile, Longarm returned his watch and derringer to his vest pockets, then retrieved his colt. Not long after, the jehu and the shotgun messenger, with the aid of the three male passengers, dragged the dead horse out from the traces and hitched one of the highwaymen's horses in its place. That chore completed, the jehu and the shotgun messenger climbed back up into the box. The passengers took their seats once more inside the stage, the whip cracked, and they resumed their journey to Harmony.

Inside the stage, Longarm handed back to Jill Dunstrom the wedding band he had retrieved from the dead highwayman. The other valuables which had been taken from the passengers had been returned earlier.

"Thank you," she murmured as she took the ring from him.

When she glanced at him, he saw fear, almost terror, in her face. He was not certain, but he thought her hand might have been trembling slightly when she reached out to take the wedding ring.

Wearily, Longarm leaned back in his seat and stared out the side window. Though they were traveling through

16

the same sunlit landscape as before, the blazing sun now seemed only to accentuate its bleak, hellish aspect. And Longarm knew why. Though his head still ached from the blow he had taken, it was not from this that his disquiet stemmed. He had just finished dealing with three road agents, two of whom he had killed. He had done so with a dread finality that had shaken Jill Dunstrom all the way down to her high-button shoes.

He guessed he didn't blame her. Just as he didn't blame the drummer and the old cattleman. They too were avoiding his eyes.

Chapter 2

The stage reached Harmony a little before midnight. Just about half the town was asleep. Pulling up in front of the Territorial House, the jehu let off his passengers, then proceeded down another block and pulled up in front of the stage company's express office.

Longarm got off at the hotel with the rest of the passengers and signed for a room on the second floor. Jill Dunstrom bid him an uneasy good-night at the desk, then hurried ahead of him up the stairs, the desk clerk carrying her baggage. Longarm picked up his own gear and hiked up to his room. He dropped his gear in a corner, then left the hotel to seek out the sheriff. He had a pretty good idea where he would find him, and he was not wrong.

The jehu and the shotgun messenger were standing beside the stagecoach talking to the sheriff. Despite the hour, a sizable crowd had already gathered around the stage. The boot was open, and a man in a long nightshirt—the undertaker, more than likely—was peering in at the two slicker-wrapped corpses. As Longarm strode up, the stage driver was doing the talking, with everyone leaning close to listen. He must have been relating Longarm's role in the botched holdup, because when he saw Longarm approaching, he said quickly to the sheriff, "Here he comes now, Tex."

The lawman swung around. In the light from the lantern outside the express office door, Longarm got a good look at the man. He was big and blocky, with a great shock of silver white hair and a drooping mustache just as snowy. Though he must have been in his late forties or early fifties, he had not allowed himself to go to seed. Big though he was, there did not appear to be an ounce of flab on his frame. His icy blue eyes were alert, the lines of his face deep. Longarm liked the breadth of his forehead and the square solidity of his chin. He got the impression at once of a man who would forge ahead, come hell or high water, if the cause was right—and maybe enjoy a few chuckles on the way.

"Name's Custis Long," Longarm told the sheriff, thrusting out his hand.

"Tex Bingham," the Sheriff replied, taking Longarm's hand and shaking it. The grasp was strong and hearty.

"Maybe we could find a place to talk?" Longarm inquired.

The sheriff nodded. "You could use a drink, I'm thinking."

Longarm did not need to reply to that.

"Let's try the Cattleman's Rest up the street here.

Their whiskey's almost fit for human consumption," said the sheriff.

Falling in beside the sheriff, Longarm said, "It's Maryland rye I'd be looking for."

"They might have it."

They found a quiet table in a corner of the saloon, and Longarm poured them each a drink from a bottle of Maryland rye. Longarm sipped it carefully and decided it would have to do. He leaned back in his chair and regarded Tex Bingham.

"You wrote the U. S. marshal about a range war. Though I would prefer it if you did not let it get around, I'm the deputy U. S. marshal he sent."

The man smiled. "I figured out who you must be when I heard how you handled the Warren boys."

"You know them?"

"They used to run cattle on the Red Ridge plateau until the Jinglebob pushed them out."

"The Mexican—you know who he is?"

"Sure. When they had a ranch to run, he was their top hand. Pedro Morales. I understand you wounded him."

Longarm nodded. "Bad."

"Think maybe I'll ride out first thing in the morning and see how the poor son of a bitch is getting along. He might bleed to death if he don't see a doctor."

"And you wouldn't want that."

"Hell, I liked the man. I didn't have anything against the Warren boys, either. Like I said in that letter, we got a range war up here, and I need help."

"Who are the parties in this range war?" Longarm asked.

"The Jinglebob and the rest of the cattlemen and farmers in this valley."

Longarm nodded. "I see."

Bingham chuckled. "I don't blame you any for what happened on that stage, Long. But it sure is strange that the gent they sent to help me quiet things down killed the only two men who were standing up to the Jinglebob."

"Tell me about this Jinglebob outfit," Longarm said.

"Harmon Dunstrom is the owner."

"Did you say Dunstrom?"

"That's right," the sheriff replied.

"Jill Dunstrom was on that stage. She married to Harmon?"

"Nope. To his brother Dennis. Or, rather, she was. Dennis is dead. He ran the Jinglebob with Harmon until he had an accident."

"But she was still wearing her wedding ring."

Bingham's smile was wintry. "She does that when she travels. Keeps off the flies."

"How did her husband die?"

"He was found chewed up pretty bad after his horse came back to the ranch one night without him. Something spooked his horse, and his boot caught in the stirrup. Before the boot came off, the poor son of a bitch had been dragged quite a ways over some very unpleasant ground."

"An accident, then."

"Maybe, maybe not. Harmon didn't think so. And from that time on he's been running roughshod over these other ranchers and the few sodbusters who are drifting in."

"You mean it became a convenient pretext for moving

against the smaller ranchers," Longarm said thoughtfully.

"That's what I mean, all right."

Longarm poured himself and the sheriff another drink. "How do you plan to stop this here range war?"

"By keeping the lid on and enforcing the law. That's why I called for help. The local town marshal is no help, and Dunstrom has tried to buy me off. When he saw he couldn't, he began making it very uncomfortable for me. I figure I'll be out after the next election, but that gives me six more months to do what I can."

Longarm looked at the sheriff carefully. "Why don't you just keep your head down until then? No one would blame you, and dogs will chase cats."

"That's not why I was hired," Bingham snapped. "There are plenty of decent citizens in this town and in the rest of James County who deserve to be protected from the lawlessness generated by Harmon Dunstrom's greed. As long as I wear this badge, I will do all I can to preserve law and order." Bingham regarded Longarm shrewdly. "I am surprised that a deputy U. S. marshal could ask such a question."

Longarm smiled. "I was just asking. By the way, my friends call me Longarm."

Bingham lifted his glass, saluted Longarm, and drank it down. Then he got up. "Get yourself some shuteye. Tomorrow morning we'll take a ride out to Pedro Morales's place. I might need someone to side me."

"That's what I'm here for."

The sheriff strode from the place. Longarm finished his drink and, taking the bottle with him, left the Cattleman's Rest and walked back to the hotel. There was still a small crowd hanging around the stage, but the two corpses were no longer resting in the boot. The onlookers grew silent, their heads turning to watch Longarm as he continued on past the stage and entered the hotel.

Up in his room, he was about ready to strip off his clothes when he heard an agitated tapping on his door. Frowning, he took his .44 from the rig hanging on the bedpost and cautiously approached the door.

"Who is it?"

"Jill Dunstrom!"

He swiftly unlocked the door and pulled it open. The young woman darted in and waited for him to close the door behind her. Turning to her, he felt a little foolish holding his big Colt.

She looked at it with some fascination, as if it were a snake gathering itself to strike. "You are a man of incredible violence," she said, her voice hushed.

"Not really, ma'am. Just careful."

He put the sixgun back in his holster and turned to her. So far he had only had time to kick off his boots. Jill Dunstrom, however, was dressed only in slippers and a long, fetching pink nightgown. Her lustrous auburn curls had been combed out, and there were two small pink ribbons in them, a perfect match for the nightgown and her glowing complexion. Her eyes held a brightness that warned Longarm.

"I am not a married woman, Mr. Long," she told him, moving suddenly closer. "I only wear that ring when I am away from Harmony and do not want any undesirable . . . involvements."

"The sheriff told me."

"You spoke of me with the sheriff. What else did he

tell you?" She was not angry, [...]
curious.

"Only how your husband died [...]

"He was murdered, Mr. Long! [...]

She took another step closer and [...]
"Today you did something I have b[...]
for the past year. You avenged me. Th[...]
you killed today were a party to my hus[...]
am almost certain of it."

"I thought it was an accident."

"Dennis had driven them from their land[...]
claim to their only water hole. They had threa[...]
kill him. I heard them. And his death occurred o[...]
they claimed as theirs. Dennis had heard they wer[...]
tling his cattle and had ridden out to warn them. [...]
Dennis did not return that night, and I never saw hi[...]
alive again."

"Did you tell all this to the sheriff?" Longarm asked.

"No."

"Don't you think you should have?"

She shook her head and gazed into his eyes. "Later,"
she murmured. And, before he could pull away, she had
flung both arms around his neck and fastened her lips to
his. He found it impossible not to respond in kind as she
propelled him backward toward the bed. The back of his
knees struck the edge of the mattress, and he fell suddenly
back, Jill Dunstrom still clinging to him.

"Ma'am . . . !" he muttered, pulling his lips free of
hers and attempting to unwind her arms from around his
neck. "There's no need for you to thank me for what I
did . . . !"

"Don't call me ma'am! You make me sound like a

25

thank you for what

?"

Do you realize

enzied way
elped her
n't she
her,
upon him,

...eg over her waist,
...wn at her. "Let me," he
...it."

...hand up across her belly and stroked
... the other breast, sliding his palm slowly
... rough texture of her nipples. Then he dropped
...mouth to them and sucked softly, then harder, oc-
casionally catching a nipple with his teeth. She cried out
in delight and began thrashing and undulating beneath
him. Pulling back, he placed his hand over her pubis and
pressed gently. The mound was already wet.

"Please," she whispered, her voice husky with desire.
"The lamp. Turn down the lamp."

When he did as she asked and returned to the bed,
she swiftly turned so that he was beneath her and she
was lying full length upon him, her naked body pressed
against his, sleek and bare to his touch from face to feet.
She locked her hands around the back of his neck and
put her mouth to his once again. When her spread thighs
pressed up against the hard length of him, the gasp that

came from her throat was so deep that at first he thought she was sobbing in anguish.

But it wasn't grief that caused her to draw up her haunches. Holding herself poised over him for just an instant, she reached back deftly and guided his erection to her pubis, then lowered herself upon him. But not all the way. Just a little of him entered her; then she pulled out and shook her head so that her long hair fell over him, cloaking him in its soft fragrance. Again she lowered herself upon him, allowing him to probe much deeper this time into her sleek moistness. Then one more time she pulled free and, letting out a soft cry, flung her head back and impaled herself on his erection, uttering a wild, shuddering moan.

She was like an animal suddenly as she began rocking back and forth, panting wildly. Reaching out, she grabbed his hair with both her hands, still rocking furiously, uttering tiny little grunting pants with each thrust. At last she flung herself full length upon him and screamed. The scream became a long, drawn-out moan, and he thought he was going to lose his hair as she writhed, trembling upon him, all the while easing him still deeper into her as if she had found a way to lock him within her forever.

"You haven't come yet, have you?" she whispered.

"That's all right," he told her, stroking her head. "It's you I'm thinking of now. You must have gone a long, long time."

"You are a gentleman. A true gentleman. But I must satisfy you. I must!"

He chuckled and rolled over onto her, pulling out just a little and sinking slowly back in again. She raised up to kiss him. Then he moved again, thrusting still deeper into her, and her head reared back, exposing the arching line of her throat. He felt power surging up from the base of his spine. Crouching on his knees, deep in her, he ran his hands up under her back to grip her shoulders and sank his teeth ever so gently into the lobe of one ear. He felt her gasp and writhe delightedly under him, her thighs thrashing open, her legs lifting up into the air around him. Locking her heels in the small of his back, her buttocks lifted off the bed with him. He reared and thrust, reared and drove, feeling that surge coming up strong and fast, driving on, continuing to thrust as he felt himself burst inside her. He fell back on his side, her legs still locked around his waist, her back arching sharply, her head rearing back, mouth open in a silent cry.

With her still quivering in his arms—her legs tucked up around him, her breasts swelling against his chest, arms tight around his body—he moved a little, still erect inside her, watching the astonishment grow in her face as he moved again, slowly, deep into her, probing her hungrily. The breath went out of her in a long exhalation as her eyes closed. Her hands gripping his back, she moved to meet his thrust.

Still moving, slowly and steadily, he kissed her gently. Her eyes opened and met his and held there, wide and dreamy, as he continued to move. He kept driving relentlessly, building fiercely now toward his second climax, no longer so much aware of her except for the wide, incredible eyes into which he seemed to be falling. And then—with a wild, drunken surge—the two of them were convulsed, clinging exultantly to each other as they came together in a single, long, shuddering exhalation.

He fell back limply, tiny nerves within him twitching slightly. He began to stroke the back of her head then, feeling the shape of her skull beneath his hands, the nape of her neck, the little ears beneath the tangle of her thick hair.

"That was nice, so nice," she said after a while.

"Yes, it was."

Resting her cheek upon his chest, she sighed deeply. "I came in to thank you, and you gave me so much more than I gave you. I feel humble."

He said nothing, just held her a bit more closely. At last she pulled away from him and rested her cheek on the heel of her palm.

Gazing wonderingly into his eyes, she said, "I do not want to let you go. You are more man than I have ever known. What is your business in Harmony, Mr. Long?"

"Call me Custis."

"Tell me, Custis. What is it?"

"I'd rather not."

She looked at him for a long moment before responding. "Now, what is that supposed to mean?"

For answer, he leaned forward and kissed her gently on the lips.

"Whatever it is you are doing, I have something more important for you," she went on urgently. "I need you to help me. I saw you with a gun today. You are the man I have been looking for—praying for. Harmon Dunstrom is cheating me. I was thinking of hiring a Pinkerton, but you would easily do as well, I am sure."

"You mean you want me to act as your range detective," Longarm said.

"Yes."

"Go on."

"I am being cheated out of my share of the Jinglebob," she told him.

"You came into your husband's share on his death."

She nodded. "I not only had a widow's rights, but Dennis had the foresight to make out a will to make sure that I received his estate."

"If it is all that ironclad, how could you be cheated?"

She laughed shortly, bitterly. "There are so many ways a partner in a ranch can be cheated. Harmon could sell beef at a higher price than he enters in his account ledger and pocket the difference. He could also sell cattle without my knowing it. Then there are the cattle on the range. How do I know which are mine? I have demanded my own brand for those cattle that are mine, but I still can't be sure Harmon is giving me my proper share— that I am alloted all the cattle that should be mine."

"You certainly don't trust Harmon," Longarm commented.

"Or his ranch hands. Harmon got rid of most of the older men, the ones Dennis hired. And he has replaced them with a mean, rough lot."

"I see. Is that all?"

"No, it's not. There is something else, Custis. Something even more terrible. Something I think only you can find out for me."

"Go on."

She looked at him for a long moment before speaking. When she did, her voice was as hard and cold as ice. "I want you to find evidence linking Harmon to the death of my husband."

Longarm was astonished. "Harmon? But, Jill, wasn't he Dennis's brother?"

"Yes, but they hated each other, and their hatred ran deep, I tell you. It frightened me at times to see them when they began goading each other. It was like two enraged bulls in a corral, each lowering its head and charging, charging repeatedly at the other."

"And Harmon's motive?"

"Control of Jinglebob, of course—complete control."

"I thought you said it was the Warrens who killed your husband."

"Harmon could have put them up to it."

He sighed. She wasn't making sense. "But, don't you see, Jill? If that were true, Harmon would not have been a party to their being driven from their holdings. How could he have dared to make them his enemies if they were involved in a murder with him?"

She smiled wickedly. "As soon as Dennis was dead and gone, Harmon gave them land. It was deep in the breaks, but they could have made use of it. It was no use, however. The Warrens had gone ugly by this time. They could not be satisfied. They wanted more. The Warrens were the only ranchers Harmon did not go after as he might have. That's why they became so bold. I tell you, they were all in it together. I'm sure of it. Harmon and the Warrens murdered my husband!"

"Why do you hate Harmon so much?" he asked.

She looked at him. "Don't you know? I live out there with him. It is only rarely that I can get away for a shopping trip to Billings or Denver. And that leaves him out there with me. Alone." She shuddered.

"Then you think..."

"That he killed his brother for me? Yes!"

"That is a pretty terrible accusation, Jill."

"Don't you think I know that? Now, will you help me?"

"With both Warrens dead, I doubt if there is anything I could find that would do any good in a court of law."

"You don't care! You refuse to help me!"

She was losing control. He pulled her close and stroked her long hair soothingly. Gradually, the tension flowed out of her and she relaxed. After a while he realized the bed was shaking. Quietly, just a little, but steadily shaking. There was no sound, but he knew she was crying.

He took her chin and lifted her face to his. The shaking stopped. "Are you all right?" he asked.

"Yes," she whispered, shuddering.

"You are filled with terrible hatred, Jill."

"I know."

"It will poison you."

"It already has—and that's why you won't help me."

"That's not it," he said.

"Then why?"

"Please believe me. I wish I could tell you."

"Tell me," she begged.

"You'll know soon enough."

She got up swiftly, snatched up her nightgown, and headed barefoot for the door. Then she came back for her slippers. Slipping them on hastily, she almost fell. He got up and held her. She turned and buried her head in his chest.

"I don't want to go back there. Don't you understand? Not to him!" she cried.

"I'll see what I can do."

She looked at him, hope flaring in her face like morning sunlight. "Will you?"

He nodded. "I can't promise anything."

"Oh, I know that!"

He smiled. She flung her arms around his neck, kissed him, then hurried out the door. He closed the door after her and listened as her light footsteps disappeared down the hallway. Then he turned wearily back to his bed and sagged onto it.

It was a foolish promise he had made, perhaps, but he did not see what harm it did to make it. If he kept his eyes and ears open, there was nothing to prevent him from finding out what he could about Harmon Dunstrom's operation—especially since he was the rancher behind the trouble brewing in James County.

He was still mulling this over when he fell into a deep, dreamless sleep.

Bright sun slanting in through his window awakened Longarm the next morning. He sat up, as famished as a wolf. Racing through his toilet, he dressed swiftly and hurried down to the lobby. He asked the desk clerk about breakfast and was directed to a small restaurant across the street. As he started from the lobby, Jill Dunstrom descended the stairs. She was delighted to see him and greeted him warmly.

Doffing his hat politely, Longarm invited her to join him for breakfast. She agreed with alacrity and a moment later the two of them were just entering the restaurant when two riders swept down Harmony's main street and pulled up beside them, raising a few pounds of dust in the process.

Frowning irritably, Jill turned to face them. Longarm turned as well. One of the riders was considerably slimmer than the other. He had pale gray eyes, and his narrow face was surprisingly sallow, his mouth weak. He had light hair and a well-trimmed, barely visible mustache. He wore his Stetson high-crowned and wore a white silk shirt under his vest. A bit of a dandy, Longarm concluded.

His companion was a heavy, thick-set mountain of a man with untidy, beetling brows, cold slits for eyes, and jowls that would have made a bulldog proud. He was heavy enough to give his horse a perpetual curvature of the spine, yet the man carried himself almost lightly as he reined in his horse and gazed down at Jill. He was wearing a large, floppy-brimmed hat, a dark, buttonless vest, and scuffed boots. His tent-sized Levi's were held up by broad yellow braces. Both men's gunbelts sagged under the weight of their gleaming, well-oiled sixguns.

"Mornin', Kelsey," Jill said to the slim rider. "Mornin', Bull," she said to his companion.

They touched their hat brims and chorused a good morning in reply. As they did so, they flicked their eyes uneasily over Longarm.

"Harmon sent us to bring you," said Kelsey. "We would've got here sooner, but Bull's horse lost a shoe."

Jill smiled thinly. "No harm done, Kelsey. We've got plenty of time. See to my spring wagon, will you? It's

34

in the livery stable. I'll be joining this gentleman for breakfast."

The two riders did not seem to like that, but they nodded obediently and rode on down the street toward the livery stable. Longarm followed Jill into the restaurant.

Kelsey, Jill explained to Longarm, was Harmon's son. Bull Schofield was the Jinglebob foreman. From the way she spoke and her manner toward them when they rode up, Longarm realized that she tolerated Kelsey but loathed Bull. When he inquired if this was so, Jill did not hesitate to confirm his suspicions.

She spoke again of the holdup, and Longarm mentioned that he and the sheriff would more than likely ride out that day to search for the wounded Mexican who had taken part in it. While he did, he would try to find out what he could about Harmon Dunstrom's operation from the sheriff. There was even the chance, he told her, that the wounded Mexican might know of any irregularities, especially if Dunstrom were selling beef illegally.

Jill did not seem as pleased as she might have at this attempt on his part to keep the promise he had made to her. But before he could remark on this, he heard the two riders they had met outside stomping into the restaurant to tell Jill the spring wagon was ready. As the men came up beside their table, she glanced coldly up at them.

"Can't you two see I am not yet finished with my breakfast? Wait outside," she ordered.

"We got work to do back at the Jinglebob," Kelsey said unhappily. "Harmon said we was to bring you back pronto. Said you should've ridden out last night, soon's the stage got in."

"He did, did he? I don't care what he said. Go on outside and wait until I have finished my breakfast."

"What's the matter, Jill?" said Bull. He spread his legs and stuck his hands into the waistband of his Levi's. He leaned close. "Ain't you had enough of this here feller?" He spoke softly, winking insolently at Longarm as he did. "That desk clerk's a real good friend of mine. He happened to notice how you didn't stay in your own room for long last night, once this here fellow checked in. Ain't fittin', you being a widow to a Dunstrom, and all. Now you come with us nice and quiet and we won't say a word to Harmon."

Jill's face went gray with shock. She glanced swiftly at Longarm. For a moment he thought she was going to be sick.

Longarm got quickly to his feet. "I guess you didn't hear Mrs. Dunstrom, Bull. Get out of here until she's finished her breakfast."

"You're a real hero, ain't you, friend? You'll find I'm a damn sight harder to finish off than them two Warrens."

"Outside, Bull," Longarm said evenly. "Now!"

"Sit down before I knock you down."

Longarm shrugged wearily. There was evidently no way out of it. This big son of a bitch was bound and determined to prove something. "If you knock me down in here, Bull, it will disturb Mrs. Dunstrom and the other patrons. I suggest we go outside."

Bull swung about and stomped from the restaurant, Longarm on his heels. As he followed Bull, Longarm had an opportunity to measure the breadth of the man's shoulders. He was not intimidated, but it did make him careful.

Bull ducked under the hitch rail and, as Longarm followed him, the man spun swiftly, even lightly for a man his size, and swung on Longarm. His big fist caught Longarm full in the mouth, instantly numbing all feeling there, slogging darkness into his brain. Bull's second punch Longarm took while rolling in closer.

By this time, the electric lust for battle had perked to life within him. Returning a sharp hook, he caught Bull on the side of his face, just under his cheekbone. The fellow rocked back, startled, then lowered his head and plowed in, thrashing at Longarm with brutal effect. They were leaning shoulder to shoulder by this time, and Longarm pumped all the power of his cool rage into these close blows, lifting Bull back each time. When they broke away, Longarm stumbled momentarily. At once he felt his skull pounded back on his shoulders by Bull's savage, lacing blows, three in thought-quick succession, all in his face.

Longarm shook off the blows and kept coming. The instinct for Bull's blood was so raw now that there was nothing the big man could do to fight off Longarm's dogged, relentless advance. Nor could he escape the hot agony of his ribs being pounded with the regularity of dripping water as Longarm's quick, knifelike fists tore through his guard and smashed wind and blood and almost the life out of him.

They had made a tight circle by this time, so that Bull's back was to the hitch rail. Bull sensed this as soon as Longarm did and stood his ground, the toes of his boots clawing into the dust. But Longarm kept jabbing, by now dodging or shunting aside Bull's slower, grunting blows on the top of his head or the edge of his shoulders, his shuffling, widespread legs taking him still closer to Bull. He could hear the slow, wheezing suck of the big man's breath as he fought to get more air into his lungs. Longarm drove in, measured him with an icy detachment, and caught him with a vicious left hook that rocked Bull back, sending him hard against the hitch rail.

Swiftly, then, Longarm moved in to deliver a series of sledging, stinging blows to the big man's head and shoulders. Each blow rocketed Bull higher and higher upon the rail until the rail cracked like a pistol shot and gave way under him. As Bull struggled to his feet and held his hands protectively up before his face, Longarm kept boring in on him. By now he was no longer aiming at Bull's body, but at the face and eyes, the jelly-like smear that was his nose. At last, when he drove his right fist through Bull's feeble guard and caught him on the shelf of his chin, he knew it was over.

Longarm followed through so completely that his arm was all the way across his body as Bull went hurtling backward through the restaurant's glass window. Longarm heard the bell-clear crash of the glass and even the hollow thud of Bull's massive head as it hit one of the tables and sent it crashing to the floor.

Longarm pulled back, aware of Sheriff Bingham standing at his side along with a silent ring of townspeople filling the street behind him. Bull did not move as he lay there peacefully on his back, his hands lying slackly at his side. There were a few shards of glass resting on his barrel of a chest, while his legs from the knees down hung out onto the sidewalk.

Longarm was still panting, his entire upper body heaving. When he tried to lift an arm to wipe the blood from his face, he knew he would have to wait until his strength returned.

Beside him, Sheriff Bingham spoke to Kelsey. "Pitch him into the wagon, Kelsey, and take Mrs. Dunstrom home."

Longarm turned his head to see Jill standing in the restaurant doorway, a look of shocked wonder on her face as she glanced from Bull's sprawled figure to Longarm. Then she hurried over to help Kelsey with Bull. Longarm swung around and pushed his way through the crowd with Bingham at his side.

"My office is over here," the sheriff told him. "There's a bottle you might sample."

Longarm grunted wearily in assent.

By the time they reached the sheriff's office, Longarm was feeling less winded. He slacked his big frame down into a hard-backed wooden chair and watched gratefully as Bingham lifted a whiskey bottle out of the bottom drawer in his desk and poured a stiff shot into a glass.

Handing it to Longarm, he said, "You mind telling me what that was all about?"

"Bull Schofield said some unpleasant things about Jill Dunstrom."

Tex nodded. "I see. And you took it upon yourself to battle for the honor of a fair lady."

Longarm smiled. "Silly, wasn't it?"

"I don't think it is ever silly to shut up a damn fool like Bull Schofield. In these parts he is known as a vicious, underhanded bully. And you are the first man

39

in this county to have stood up to him."

"It wasn't easy."

Tex smiled. "It don't look like it was, at that. One thing's for sure. You've evened things up nicely, Longarm. You had the small ranchers lined up against you when you wiped out the Warrens. Despite being driven off their land by Dunstrom, they had hung around and were doing their best to stand up to Jinglebob. Of course, now we all know where they were getting the money to do so. But that don't matter. At least they stood up to Dunstrom. And now you've got Jinglebob, the biggest ranch in the county, ranked against you on the other side. You sure as hell are impartial."

Longarm threw the hot liquid down his throat and felt its warmth stir through his belly clear to his fingertips. He smiled, aware for the first time of his thick, unresponsive lips. "You mean I'm just like you," he said. "Squarely in the middle."

Tex nodded soberly. "That's about it."

"Give me a few minutes and we'll ride out to see about Pedro Morales."

Shaking his head in wonder, Bingham stoppered the bottle and put it back into his desk. Then he got up and slapped Longarm on the back. There was no way he could hide the fact. Tex Bingham liked Longarm, and Longarm found himself returning the warmth.

And that was one hell of a thing. Suppose the chief was right—and Tex Bingham really was Bart Bonham, the man who had bushwhacked Charlie Vail?

Chapter 3

Before they could leave the sheriff's office, the town marshal stormed in, his face red. "What in tarnation's goin' on here, Tex?" he blustered angrily.

"Now, don't let your bowels get into an uproar, Slim. Long and I, we've got everything under control," Bingham replied.

The town marshal was a smallish fellow with a peaked, bony face and washed-out hazel eyes that seemed unable to remain still. He wore a high-peaked gray Stetson, Levi's, a checked shirt, and a black, buttonless vest. His boots were cheap-looking and scuffed raw. There was a dusty air of indigence about him. He was loaded down with two gleaming, pearl-handled Colts, which did not look as if they had ever been fired.

"Damn it, Bingham!" Slim cried. "You don't seem

to understand. Bull Schofield's just been hauled out of town in a spring wagon. There's goin' to be hell to pay, now we got Jinglebob's dander up. We got to be prepared! Harmon will send in his boys to rattle this here feller's teeth. And maybe they'll shoot up the town!"

"The world ain't comin' to an end, Slim," Bingham told him, the ghost of a smile on his face. "Simmer down. You sound like Henny Penny."

"Henny Penny? Who the hell's that?"

Longarm grinned at the disturbed town marshal. "Why, you must know her," he explained patiently. "She's the chicken kept insisting the sky was falling."

"I don't know anything about her," the man said, uncomprehending. "All I know is we got to get ready for Harmon and his boys." He stared unhappily at Longarm. "And you, sir, I suggest you get out of town fast. There's a stage leaving by noon."

"Much obliged," said Longarm.

"You can go now, Slim," Bingham said wearily. "We got business."

The town marshal stared at Bingham for a minute, flung an unhappy glance at Longarm, then ducked back out of the office. The sound of his hurrying feet disappeared swiftly.

Bingham looked wearily at Longarm. "Now you see what kind of help I got to side me. It was Harmon Dunstrom got that fellow elected town marshal—and the fellow he's grooming to take *my* place you just sent through a restaurant window."

Longarm and Bingham rode out of Harmony not long after, heading for the low, pine-clad hills about five miles distant, where Pedro Morales was supposed to have settled when he lost his job at the Warren ranch. Longarm was riding a dapple-gray and the sheriff a big chestnut, both of which they had rented from the livery stable.

As the sun lifted in the east, Longarm felt its warmth fall upon his sore frame and was grateful. The exhilaration of the battle was gone now, leaving him to deal with its nagging side effects and unpleasant reminders, especially the soreness about his ribs and the odd numbness of his upper lip.

Harmony dwindled behind them to one or two scattered houses and a few corrals, and then they rode for a while alongside the meandering shallows of a mountain-fed stream, following a rutted wagon trail that cut down the middle of the valley. Low hills, perhaps five miles apart, formed the walls of the valley, and at least ten miles ahead was a low line of buttes which effectively sealed off the valley from the west.

Cowbirds lifted in thick flights from the river willows. It was lush, rich land, ideal for cattle, and securely locked away from the world. Along the flat stretch Longarm saw close herds of tallow-heavy beef, standing sometimes in grass up to their snouts. A few miles from Harmony a narrower road turned to the left, crossed a bridge, and struck for the northern ridge. They turned onto it and began to lift into higher country.

The two men rode in silence, alternately at a walk and a gallop, the smell of the earth pleasantly rising to Longarm's nostrils and the sweet, crisp air filling his sore chest. There was an ease and a rhythm in his muscles while he rode, and his senses lifted as the bright morning awakened about them. He was sure as hell out of the stink of Denver now, and this was what he had been craving, the action he had to have, this hard-packed trail running beneath his horse's hooves and the steady thudding rhythm of the dapple-gray's stride pulsing through his solid frame.

An hour passed in this fashion, then another. By midmorning they were deep in the hills that crowded upon the northern flanks of the valley when they reached a canyon with sheer walls and width enough to let only a narrow stream and an even narrower trail pass through it. The mouth of the canyon was shadowed until the canyon widened and the trail became a road again, tracing its way between the shoulders of broken hill country. They continued to climb and by noon they were closed in by timber, still climbing steadily, when they topped a pine-covered ridge and pulled up.

Behind them, lost in the midday haze, was the valley. Only portions of it were visible now between sheer walls and shouldering hills. The river, slicing its center, from this height was but a slim gleaming meander. Before them lay the ridges and wooded peaks of broken country, dark with timber, undulating like heavy sea swells northward until the choppy land subsided against the vaulting walls of rock face and scrub pine.

They left the ridge and followed a narrow trail that took them through cool shadows and deep silence except for the haunting calls of the wood thrush echoing in the timbered slopes hanging above them. An hour or so later they came out upon a stumpy clearing in the midst of which sat a small log cabin and a lean-to which served as a barn. The chimney was only half finished, the roof—patched raggedly with tar paper—was sagging dangerously, and the door hung open on leather hinges. So high were the weeds about the place that Longarm could only just make out the corrals. Amidst all this natural loveliness, the cabin reminded Longarm once again of the curse of human habitation.

"This is Pedro's place, Longarm," the sheriff said, pulling up. "But I don't see any smoke coming from that chimney."

"It looks deserted, sure enough."

Longarm urged his mount on down the slope, the sheriff following. When they reached the cabin, they reined in their mounts.

"Hello, the house!" Longarm called.

The silence that greeted this call was almost oppressive.

The two men dismounted and walked up onto the low front porch, where grass sprouted between the warped boards. Longarm glanced through the open doorway into the cabin's interior. He could see where stray cattle had made a shelter of the place and had scrubbed themselves against the door frame. A crude stairway ran up along one side of the room. Then he saw a fireplace. Frowning, he looked closer and saw the smouldering coals of a recent fire. Sniffing at the air, he caught the faint odor of wood smoke.

He pulled back from the window and was about to point this out to the sheriff when from behind them came a sharp, angry woman's voice: "Drop your guns, Sheriff," she said. "You, too, mister."

Longarm and Bingham swung around to see a Mexican woman approaching from the pines above the clearing, a Winchester in her hands. From the ease with which she carried it, it was obvious that she knew how to use it. Moving slowly, Longarm reached in for his Colt and dropped it carefully on the soft ground beyond the porch.

"Damn!" muttered Bingham, unbuckling his own gunbelt. "Where in hell did she come from? Never heard tell Pedro had a woman up here."

Longarm could understand why Pedro might have kept this woman entirely to himself. Indeed, it was startling to see a woman dressed as she was this far north. Though her raven-black hair was hidden almost entirely by a white *rebozo* or head scarf, her brightly colored skirt—rust-colored with green bands and trimmed with heavy black thread—barely covered her knees, and her blouse was cut low, revealing the dark cleft between her heavy breasts, and as far as Longarm could make out, the woman wore nothing beneath her flaring skirt. To any American, such a happy disregard for the strictures of a decent woman's attire would be an incitement to riot, which was obviously why Pedro had kept this woman of his hidden away in these hills.

"Who're you?" Bingham asked her as she pulled up in front of them.

"I am Maria, Pedro's woman. Why do you come here?"

"We're looking for Pedro," the sheriff told her.

She accepted that without a flicker of her dark eyes. Then she stepped aside and, turning, indicated the pines she had just quit with her rifle barrel.

"He is up there," she told them. "Waiting for you, I think."

Bingham glanced at Longarm and shrugged. Longarm nodded. The sheriff started across the yard for the pines,

46

Longarm beside him. The woman kept a few careful strides behind them. Once in the pines, they found a dim pathway leading between the fragrant aisles and kept going until they had topped a ridge.

Pulling up, they saw just over the ridge a line shack built into a low shelf fronted with huge boulders, its sides bolstered with sod, its roof heavy with pine boughs. A pale white tracery of wood smoke lifted from its field-stone chimney. The shack looked solid enough to withstand even a Montana winter. Longarm understood at once. The decaying cabin in the clearing below acted as a decoy to lure unsuspecting posse members.

Maria came up behind Longarm and prodded him none too gently to keep him going toward the line shack. When they reached the shack and entered, they found Pedro lying on a bunk set along the far wall. He had a big pillow under his head and was staring up at the ceiling. His swarthy face seemed unnaturally pale. At their entrance he just barely managed to turn his head in their direction.

The moment Pedro saw Longarm, he swore and attempted to push himself upright. *"Diablo!"* he muttered hoarsely, shaking an accusing finger at Longarm. "Fool! You spoil everything. You not understand! Is not what you think..."

Startled, Maria glanced with narrowed eyes at Longarm, then addressed Pedro in Spanish. He lay back down and, staring up at the ceiling, spoke to her in a feeble, despairing voice. When he had finished, Maria turned to Longarm, her face cold and implacable. Levering a fresh cartridge into the Winchester's firing chamber, she moved carefully back a step and leveled the rifle on his chest.

"Outside, mister," she told Longarm. Glancing at Bingham, she snapped, "You, too, Sheriff."

"What are you going to do, Maria?" Bingham asked.

"I will kill this one. He has kill Pedro. He make big mistake, but I will not make a mistake."

"You do that and you hang," the sheriff told her.

"Get out of here," Maria snapped, moving the rifle menacingly, "or I kill you while Pedro watch!"

Longarm walked out of the line shack ahead of the sheriff. Using the sheriff's blocky body to hide the motion of his right hand, he started to reach into his vest pocket for the .44 derringer. But the moment he lowered his right hand, Maria darted out to one side and snarled at him to keep his hand away from his body.

Longarm stopped and turned to face Maria, and the sheriff did likewise.

"What is it, Maria?" Longarm demanded. "What is Pedro talking about? He and the Warrens tried to hold up the stage. If Pedro got wounded in the attempt, what else could either of you have expected?"

"Holdup!" she snapped angrily. "That was no holdup!"

She lifted her rifle higher to be more sure of her aim and sighted along the barrel at Longarm.

"No, Maria!" Bingham cried. "You can't! This is murder!"

She turned on him in a fury, clubbing him with the rifle barrel. In that instant Longarm flung himself to the right, reaching into his vest for his derringer as he did so. He struck the ground hard and heard the sheriff crying out dimly as Longarm scrambled to his feet and began to crab frantically for the cover of nearby rocks.

Maria's rifle cracked and a slug whined off a rock inches from his head. Frantically unclipping the derringer from his watch chain, he dove behind a rock. Pulling his feet in behind him, he swung his derringer around. Maria fired again. This time a spray of rock particles burst so close to his face that he had to duck swiftly away to protect his eyes.

He saw Pedro staggering out of the shack behind Maria and the sheriff lying flat on the ground, his hat a few feet from his sprawled body. Weaponless, the man was lying there, still conscious, cursing. Pedro, leaning on the doorframe, leveled a sixgun at the sheriff and fired. Longarm saw a plume of dirt explode inches from Bingham's head and threw a round at Pedro. Pedro staggered back and slipped to one knee.

Screaming out her rage at Longarm, Maria began pumping furiously on the lever of her Winchester, sending a murderous spray of slugs into the rocks where Longarm was crouching. He had only one more round left in his derringer, and Maria was not giving him a chance to poke his head up to aim the weapon.

Abruptly, a fusillade of shots came from the rocks above and behind Longarm. He saw Maria go slamming back, the rifle flying from her grasp. Pedro, on his hands and knees, began to crawl toward her, but another brutal fusillade cut him down even as he reached out to the woman.

Maria was not dead. She stirred and began to crawl toward Pedro. Two more quick, efficient rifle shots sang out again from above Longarm and Maria was flung brutally to one side. Another shot struck her still body and Longarm saw her blouse jump where the round entered. A thin, pathetic gout of fresh blood pulsed from this last wound, and Maria did not stir again.

Groaning with the horror of it, Sheriff Bingham pushed himself slowly erect, his glance searching the rocks above Longarm. Getting to his feet also, Longarm looked up at the rough slope.

"Who's up there?" he cried.

But there was no reply. Still holding the derringer, Longarm clambered up the slope toward the ledge from where he thought the rifle shots might have come. Before he reached it, he heard the sudden clatter of hooves, and by the time he got to the ledge, the sound was replaced by the haunting sighing of the wind high in the pines. Behind him, the sheriff came into view.

"Who was it?" he asked.

"I don't know."

Longarm caught the gleam of spent cartridges in the short grass. He bent and picked them up, then handed them to Bingham.

"A Winchester, .44-40," the man said quickly as he examined them briefly and flung them back to the ground. "Whoever it is, you owe him your life."

"I guess that's true enough. But who the hell was it?" Longarm asked.

"Never look a gift horse in the mouth."

"Maybe," Longarm said. "But, then again, maybe this is one time I should check out the gift horse. There's something about this I don't like."

"You mean, why didn't our benefactor stay around to identify himself?"

"That's what I mean, all right."

The sheriff rubbed the side of his neck where the girl had struck him, and sighed. "She was a wild one, that woman. I guess she really loved her man."

"And he loved her."

"I guess we better go ahead and bury them."

Longarm nodded and followed the sheriff back down through the rocks to the line shack.

It was a grim, silent business they had to perform. The only shovel they could find was in poor condition, its blade bent and dull. They wrapped the bodies in bedsheets, then tugged and sweated as they lifted, then dropped them into the two shallow trenches they had dug out of the grim, unyielding soil. To protect the bodies from wolves, they piled rocks over the graves until they had a low but solid cairn to mark their final resting place. It seemed all wrong to Longarm that these two should die like this, so far from the hot, dusty land from which they had come.

He took his hat off and studied the grave for a moment, then slapped it back on and headed for his horse. As the two mounted up, Bingham nudged his horse closer.

"You sure you want to do this?" he asked.

Longarm nodded. "We came out here to see about the Mexican. We got two corpses instead, courtesy of a rifleman who preferred to shoot and run. I want to know why."

"Be careful. This is a tough land. This is where the nesters and small ranchers fighting Jinglebob have been pushed. They feel crowded and have a tendency to shoot

51

first and ask questions after."

"Thanks for the warning, Sheriff. Now go on back and see if you can calm Slim down before he has a heart attack."

Grinning wryly at Longarm's thrust, Bingham touched his hat brim in salute and turned his horse around to ride back the way he had come. Longarm watched him for a moment, then turned his horse the other way, to the north, the direction in which he had heard those pounding hooves disappear.

Longarm soon lost track of the sign left by that single rifleman, but he kept going anyway, determined to find out what he could before returning to Harmony. About two hours later he discovered he was being tailed. Twice as he glanced back at a ridge paralleling his route, he caught the flash of sunlight on a gun barrel.

Spotting a ranch off to his right in among some hills, he decided to make for it. By then he was deep in a rugged, hardscrabble country that would not graze one head to forty acres, if Longarm was any judge. Turning his mount off the seldom traveled road he had been following, he pushed through a sagging gate and kept on toward the ranch. The main building was a log cabin set into the ground with no porch. Rickety sheds adjoined the cedar-pole corral and in the middle of the barn lot was a rusting cultivator. The place spoke of poverty, shiftlessness, and indifference.

He was almost to the house when a bone-thin fellow stepped through the open door, a rifle cradled in his arm. He was tall, unshaven, and dressed in a torn undershirt and ragged, patched Levi's. His boots were split, Longarm saw. He stood there hatless, his bald head scalded red by the sun.

"That's far enough!" he told Longarm.

Longarm reined in his mount. "That rifle ain't very neighborly," he said mildly.

"You ain't a neighbor." The fellow sniffed and took a hesitant step closer. "Who're you, and what are you doin' on my land?"

"Just passin' through. I'm a mite thirsty and my horse could use water."

"You ain't told me yet who you are," the man insisted.

"Name's Long. Custis Long. I arrived in Harmony last night on the stage."

"You're a long ride from Harmony."

Longarm did not see that he had to comment on that. He folded his arms and waited. The rancher could either send him on his way or invite him to light and set a spell. It didn't really matter all that much which it was.

"All right, then," the fellow said warily. "Light. My girl's got some coffee on. You can tend to your horse and set a spell, if you've a mind."

Longarm off-saddled the dapple-gray, watered it out of a bucket beside the well he found on the other side of the barn, then trudged into the house. When he entered, he found himself in a dim, dirt-floored cabin. The windows were small and there weren't enough of them. The result was an oppressive dimness.

Slumping onto a rough bench pulled up in front of a deal table, he saw a young woman of twenty or so turn from the stove, a steaming pot of coffee in her hand. As she filled the tin cup in front of him, she brushed a wisp of hair off her forehead.

"I don't have no doughnuts," she said. "Or rolls. This coffee will have to do."

"It will do nicely, ma'am," Longarm told her. "Thank you."

His manners surprised her and she pulled back, mollified. It was obvious she had been somewhat irritated at her father for having invited him in. She was fairskinned with thick, curly, almost raven-black hair. Her eyes were a startling blue, her lips full, a dark red flower against her flawless complexion. Though she was dressed in a formless shift she had fashioned from the poorest cloth, she wore it with simplicity and grace.

"This here is Kitty, my daughter, Mr. Long," the man said with obvious pride. "My name is Wilkinson. Clyde Wilkinson."

"Much obliged, Clyde," Longarm said, sipping the coffee.

"You got business around here?" Clyde asked carefully.

Longarm shrugged. "Thought I might buy me some land, do some ranching, settle down. But this sure as hell is bleak country."

"Bleak ain't the half of it," Kitty replied, standing back and peering at Longarm. "But it's our land and we aim to keep it, come hell or high water."

"You don't mean anyone is trying to take it from you, do you?"

"Jinglebob wants it," she told him indignantly, again brushing the lock of hair off her forehead. "And maybe you're working for the son of a bitch."

"Ma'am, I am not working for Jinglebob. I've sure heard about it. But I am just one man looking over the valley and these hills. How come you're so all fired up about that ranch?" Longarm asked.

"Because Jinglebob wants all the land in this here valley, that's why," she said bitterly. "And he ain't particular how he gets it."

Her father started to agree, but began coughing instead. He slammed the cup of coffee down on the table and grabbed the edge of the table for support. It was a terrible, grinding spasm that appeared to be ripping his insides out. Kitty had rushed to his side instantly. Bending over him, Kitty felt his forehead and then glanced imploringly at Longarm.

"Help me with him!" she cried. "I can't manage him any more!"

"What do you want me to do?" Longarm asked, jumping to his feet and circling the table.

"Help me get him into his bedroom."

Longarm pushed gently past the girl and lifted the man out of his seat as easily as if he had been an oversized rag doll. He was so light that Longarm was appalled. The girl darted ahead of him into the bedroom, struck a match, and lit the lamp to give him light, then stood aside as he laid the old man gently down on the cot. Clyde Wilkinson was no longer coughing, but he was wheezing painfully, his eyes wide. His open mouth looked like a ragged hole someone had punched into a slab of bread dough.

Gradually the man's wheezing subsided and some hint of color returned to his cheeks. Kitty straightened and looked at Longarm.

"He'll be all right, I reckon. He just needs rest. He was lying down when you rode up."

Longarm turned and left the room. Kitty blew out the lamp and followed him from the room, quietly closing the door behind her. Longarm returned to his coffee and Kitty sat down beside him, her forehead resting on the heel of her hand.

He could tell that she was about at the end of her rope. From the looks of it, both of them were.

Longarm finished his coffee and then leaned back in his chair, fixing her with a hard, questioning gaze. "There's a rider on my tail," Longarm told her, "and your father left his sickbed to meet me at the door with a rifle in his hand. And Jinglebob is behind it all, you say. Maybe you can tell me why. This land is too poor to be fought over with such bitterness. I don't understand it."

"It ain't just the land, Mr. Long."

"What do you mean?"

"It's Harmon Dunstrom's big plans," Kitty said.

"Plans for what? A cattle empire? You can't run cattle if you don't have the grass for it, and I've seen precious little grass in these hills."

"Have you been to Red Notch yet?"

"Where in hell is it?"

"A few miles north of here."

"I should reach it by nightfall, then. How big a town is it?" he asked.

"Not very big. It used to be a stage station before the railroad came."

"So what is it now?"

"A slaughterhouse—or it will be soon."

"Did I hear you right?" Longarm asked.

She nodded wearily.

"You mean he's going to slaughter and dress cattle way the hell out here and ship them east?"

"That's his plan. Yes."

Longarm leaned back in his chair and took a deep breath. Of course! This was why Harmon Dunstrom was after every bit of ranching land he could get his hands on and why he didn't want anyone else in on his scheme. If he owned all the land and ran all the cattle, he would make money both ways, growing beef and selling it. He would be eliminating the middleman. And there would be no more need for trail drives.

"To build a slaughterhouse out here would take a fortune, Kitty. I've heard of a few Easterners trying such a thing, but so far nothing has come of it."

"I think the railroad is investing in it, too," she told him.

"How come you know all this?"

"An engineer Dunstrom hired stopped by here one day. He told us everything."

"What happened to him? I'd like to talk to him."

"You won't have much luck," Kitty said.

"Why not?"

She looked at him bleakly. "He disappeared."

Longarm considered that a moment. The poor son of a bitch was probably killed so he wouldn't let any more cats out of the bag. "How many others know about this slaughterhouse?" he asked.

"My father and I told all the farmers and ranchers around here, but I don't think anyone in Harmony knows yet."

"You're right. The sheriff doesn't know, I'm sure. How far has Dunstrom got with this grand scheme of his?"

"From what I heard, there hasn't been much work done on the slaughterhouse, not since that engineer disappeared. That poor fellow! He didn't think Dunstrom could do it. He said Harmon would have to slaughter at least twenty thousand head a season to make a profit this far from the eastern markets."

"That's a lot of beef," said Longarm.

Kitty nodded glumly. "Now you see why he wants the entire valley."

"Yes, I do."

"But we ain't standing still. My dad's a lawyer, and he's organizing all ranchers and farmers. Harmon's bought up four farmers and scared off two small ranchers already, but he's not having much luck with the rest."

"And your father's behind that. He's the one leading the fight."

Kitty nodded unhappily, glancing toward the bedroom as she did so. They were both thinking the same thing, Longarm knew. How could a man in such poor health really lead an organization that was trying to stop a power like Harmon Dunstrom?

"You say your father's a lawyer, Kitty. What is he doing out here in these badlands?" Longarm asked.

She smiled sadly. "Dad's a dreamer, Mr. Long. He thought these wide-open spaces would be good for his health."

"And instead the hard work only tore it down more."

She nodded miserably. "Dad had no idea what it would take to run in these hills. No idea at all. He tried to plant

58

a crop last year, wheat and corn, to sell to the other ranchers for fattening their stock. There was no rain, and then what rain there was washed the seedlings into the gulleys. We are finished here, Mr. Long."

"Except that you don't have any money to finance a move elsewhere."

She nodded.

"And your father is too stubborn to admit defeat."

She looked at him with glum appreciation. "That's Dad, all right."

"So he's leading a charge against Harmon. Can he count on the other ranchers and farmers to back him when push comes to shove?"

"I can't answer that."

Longarm got to his feet and smiled down at Kitty. "I guess I'll keep on riding. I should reach Red Notch before sundown."

Kitty rose to her feet and walked with him to the door. Pausing in the doorway, Longarm glanced swiftly about at the dark hills, wondering if that rider was still out there, waiting for him to continue his journey. And wondering too what the rider would decide to do when Longarm reached Red Notch. There was always the chance that this was the same rider who had cut down Pedro and Maria, but Longarm doubted it. He was almost certain that the man tailing him was a Jinglebob rider, sent by Harmon to keep an eye on this stranger who had already mussed up his future sheriff.

He pushed out into the yard and saddled up his dapple-gray. Kitty went with him, watching without comment as he worked. He knew she appreciated his company and was probably wishing he would stay longer. He checked the cinch one more time, then vaulted easily into the saddle and looked down at the girl.

Her pale beauty seemed so frail now against the dark, lowering hills surrounding them that he felt a pang at the thought of leaving her in this bleak, unhappy situation. But she and her father had survived so far, and were now, in fact, leading the other ranchers and farmers against the Jinglebob.

"Thanks for the coffee, Kitty," he told her, "and my regards to your father."

"You are welcome, Mr. Long. If that rider trailing you is a Jinglebob hand, be careful."

"I will," he said.

She stepped back and he nudged his mount about and rode out of the yard. Before he reached the gate he glanced back and saw her still standing in the yard. He waved, and she waved back.

Chapter 4

Red Notch was a quiet town that seemed to have stirred fitfully from a deep sleep not too long ago, then fallen back into a troubled, uncertain slumber.

On one side of the single main street under a heavy stand of cottonwoods lay a tangle of cedar-pole corrals and a long adobe building which had served as the town's stage station and saloon. Behind the stage station, its surface gleaming through the cottonwoods, was the same broad stream Longarm had followed for a while on his ride out of Harmony.

Three large adobe buildings sat across from the stage station. A two-story frame hotel and train station had been constructed next to these, and as Longarm rode closer he caught the gleam of rails in the setting sun. They ran out of the northwest and cut past the station, heading for the notch in the pine-clad hills to the east. Longarm saw that it was only a feeder line at best, and so far it had not appeared to have done much for the town's prosperity.

But Harmon Dunstrom appeared to be doing everything he could to remedy that. Behind the hotel on a broad flat at least two hundred yards distant were neat piles of lumber and brick, great rough pyramids of barrels, portable work sheds and wagons. Most but not all of this equipment and material was covered by heavy tarpaulins. Large, rectangular excavations had been dug out of the ground for the foundations of the slaughterhouse and its support buildings, the exposed ground gaping raw in the slanting sunlight. But the excavations appeared abandoned, their edges weathering and in many cases worn away like the teeth of an old Indian.

As he approached the saloon, Longarm squinted through the sunset of a sorry-looking team hitched to a buckboard in front of it, with two saddle horses alongside. Pulling his mount to a halt beside the buckboard, he dismounted, stiff from the long day's ride, and turned casually to gaze back along the trail he had just ridden over. The rider who was tailing him was no longer making any effort to stay concealed. He stood out clearly against the salmon-colored sky as he rode into Red Notch.

Longarm dropped his reins over the hitch rail and tramped up onto the saloon's porch and through the door. Stepping into the dim, dirt-floored room, he paused for a moment to let his eyes get accustomed to the gloom. As he did so, all conversation in the place died. On the right was a rough-deal bar at which three men were standing. The bartender was a scarecrow of a man with

62

strands of greased black hair plastered straight back over his pale skull. He wore no shirt over his dirty underwear. Broad, greasy-looking galluses held up his pants. At the far end of the room canned goods and bottles were racked in a halfhearted attempt at display.

Under the stares of the three customers Longarm moved over to the bar, thumbed his hat off his forehead, and asked for whiskey. The bartender set out a shotglass and bottle for him and Longarm slowly poured a drink. The three customers resumed their conversation, but they spoke so softly that Longarm heard only an occasional word. As he drank he noticed how quickly the three men tossed down their drinks, paid up, and filed out of the place.

When the rattle of the departing buckboard and the clatter of the two saddle horses died, a nervous, waiting silence hung in the air. The bartender kept glancing uneasily at Longarm. The silence was broken at last by the steady, rhythmic hoofbeats of an approaching rider. As the horseman pulled up outside the saloon, Longarm took his bottle and shotglass over to a table against the wall and sat down to wait.

After a moment the doorway was darkened as the tallest fellow Longarm had seen outside of a circus entered and paused momentarily. So tall was the man that he had to stoop as he came in. He was dressed in clerical black, with a wide, floppy-brimmed hat, dark trousers, and highly polished boots. His sidearm was worn high on his right hip, the holster and pistol grip hidden by the skirts of his long frock coat.

As big as he was tall, the man was clean-shaven, with a solid, heavy line for a mouth and a square jawline. His face was as brown and gnarled as polished oak. His hair was as light as his son Kelsey's, and he wore it long, almost to his shoulders. His nose was hooked and prominent, his eyes commanding. As he paused in the doorway he radiated raw, brute power. If a grizzly had been turned human and set loose, that creature would be the one standing at that moment in the saloon doorway.

The bartender ran his hand nervously over his pale skull. "Evenin', Harmon," he said. "The usual?"

Harmon Dunstrom nodded and stepped all the way into the saloon. His eyes had been on Longarm from the moment he had entered. As the barkeep brought a bottle around the bar, Harmon strode over to Longarm's table and paused before it, his presence hovering over it like a malign cloud.

"Mind if I join you?" he asked with surprising gentleness.

Longarm shrugged. "Sit down."

As the barkeep placed Harmon's bottle and a shotglass down on the table, the owner of the Jinglebob pulled a chair over and sat down carefully. Reaching for the bottle, he poured himself a drink, threw it down his gullet, then filled the shotglass a second time and set it down before him. Turning the shotglass slowly, he glanced up at Longarm. "I been following you."

"I know."

"Who the hell are you, mister?" Dunstrom asked.

"Custis Long."

"You heard me, damn it. Who the hell are you?"

Longarm shrugged. "I just told you."

"Damn you to hell," Harmon said softly, his voice rumbling like distant thunder. "You ride in on that stage

64

and kill two local ranchers before you even reach town. Then you wipe the street up with my foreman. After that you ride out to that fool, Wilkinson, an asshole who thinks he can rally the ranchers and sodbusters against me. What the hell are you up to, Long?"

Longarm decided this was his year to be cagey. "Think carefully, Dunstrom. Those two local ranchers were holding up the stage. They deserved to be shot. And that foreman of yours insulted Jill Dunstrom, your sister-in-law, in my company. And sure I stopped at Clyde Wilkinson's place just now. I needed a place to rest my horse and set a spell. Simmer down, why don't you?"

"I been on your tail for some time now."

"I know that."

"Where were you coming from when I picked up your trail?" Dunstrom asked. "I didn't see the sheriff with you, but I know you left Harmony with him this morning."

"The sheriff's on his way back to Harmony."

"Back from where?"

"From the third road agent's cabin, the one I wounded."

Dunstrom leaned back in his chair and studied Longarm closely. "You mean the sheriff is bringing him in?"

"Afraid not. We just got through burying him and his woman."

Longarm studied Dunstrom's face for any sign that he knew what had happened at the Mexican's place. But Dunstrom's face revealed nothing but surprise at Longarm's words.

"You mean the Mex fought back when you went for him?" the rancher asked.

"That's right."

65

Dunstrom appeared to be simmering down. He reached for his drink and sipped it reflectively. Then he looked sharply at Longarm.

"I don't mind telling you, I am doing all I can to get rid of that meddling Sheriff Bingham. There's an election coming up and I was thinking of replacing him with my foreman. But maybe Bull Schofield ain't the right man for the job."

Longarm carefully poured himself a drink. He had an idea what Dunstrom was driving at, and was wondering what his own response should be.

"How would you like to be the next sheriff of James County?" Dunstrom asked.

Longarm looked at Dunstrom. "You that sure you can deliver the votes in this county, as easy as that?"

"I am the law in this county. I can deliver anything I want. I can *do* anything I want. And no shortsighted son of a bitch in a tin star is going to stop me from developing this valley the way I see fit."

"And just how do you plan to develop this valley?" Longarm asked.

"You mean Wilkinson didn't tell you?"

"He told me."

"I admit the project is not going so well at the moment. I am having trouble getting the additional range I need, but that won't last. I am willing to pay for what I want, Long."

"You mean if I became sheriff, I wouldn't have to live on a couple of hundred dollars a month."

"That's right." The rancher leaned back suddenly. The chair groaned under the sudden shift of weight. "What do you say?" he asked.

"I couldn't do it, Dunstrom."

"Why not, damn it?"

"I already got a job."

Dunstrom's eyes narrowed. "What is it?"

"I am a deputy U. S. marshal. Sheriff Bingham sent to Washington for help to stop this here war you're waging against your neighbors." Longarm smiled. "I would've told you sooner, but I wanted to hear what you had to say."

"You son of a bitch!"

"I should ask you to take that back, but I already had one fight today. Besides, you're bigger than I am," Longarm said mildly.

"In more ways than one, Marshal."

"Why don't you forget this pipe dream, Dunstrom? Forget about putting up a slaughterhouse out here in the middle of nowhere. Be a good neighbor to the other ranchers in this valley and live in peace. Then I can go back to Denver, and you won't have to worry about who's sheriff in James County."

"No," the rancher said fiercely.

"Why?"

"I've already been driven from my last spread by lousy, two-bit ranchers and grubby sodbusters who only know how to overgraze their pastures or tear up the grasslands and leave it to the wind and sun. This here is my last stand, Marshal. When I die, my boy Kelsey is going to have something he can build on. Maybe you can understand that. Maybe you can't. This here is cattle country, and I have made me a nice deal with the railroad for that slaughterhouse. All I have to do now is guarantee them enough dressed beef to make it profitable."

"Buy the beef from the other ranchers. Maybe some of these sodbusters could put up pens and begin topping off your beef. They could grow corn. Work with them, not against them, Dunstrom. Then the entire valley could prosper, not just Jinglebob."

Harmon looked at Longarm with grudging respect. "Hell, man, don't you think I thought of that? And then I saw what I had to work with. These ranchers and nesters won't work with me or anyone else. They want to scruff along from day to day, year after year, on their own hook. They are too goddamned independent—and proud of it. I can't wait for them to change, Marshal. I ain't getting any younger."

Longarm shrugged. "What you are saying is that if they won't go along, you will make them."

"That's what I'm saying."

"Sheriff Bingham and I will do everything we can to stop you."

Harmon got to his feet. "I can't allow that, Marshal."

"There's nothing you can do to stop us, nothing legal, that is. I'm only one federal marshal. Stop me and there will be others. You can't fight the entire federal government."

"I can if I do it right, Marshal."

Dunstrom turned and strode from the saloon. Longarm watched him go with a weary sense that, as certainly as thunder followed lightning, bad trouble was on the way. Harmon Dunstrom was as wrong and as bullheaded as a man could be, but he was big enough and tough enough to cause all the trouble he contemplated, and then some. It didn't really matter if a man was right sometimes. All that mattered was for him to think he was. Jefferson

Davis sure as hell could give a lecture on that subject.

Longarm heard Dunstrom ride off, poured himself another drink, then got up from the table, paid the bartender for the bottle, and left the saloon. The sun had vanished below the enclosing hills, leaving the world as black as the inside of a whore's heart. The hotel across the street had a light on in the lobby, and when he led his horse across the street to it, he saw the entrance to a small livery stable in back. He found a very old, stove-up cowboy behind the front desk, who assured him he would see to his horse.

Upstairs on the second floor, Longarm checked his room out and only decided to use it when he saw that one of his room's windows opened out onto a narrow, side porch roof. The whiskey, coming on an empty stomach, had left him a mite light-headed. He lay down on the bed without bothering to kick off his boots or take off his cross-draw rig. He could telegraph for help, he supposed. But what would he tell Billy? A man shouldn't call for help until he was truly threatened. And so far, all Harmon had done was to tell Longarm what he planned to do if he wanted to build that slaughterhouse.

Longarm closed his eyes, crossed his arms under his head, and let himself drift off to an uneasy sleep.

He awoke to the dim clatter of horsemen entering Red Notch. He got to his feet instantly and went to the window. Six riders swept into town from the west and clattered up to the saloon. One rider dismounted and entered the place. Coming out a second later, he mounted up and led the other riders down the street to the hotel. Longarm recognized the rider who had dismounted. It was Bull Schofield, determined to redeem himself in his sovereign's eye, Longarm had no doubt.

Before going to sleep, Longarm had dropped his hat on the floor beside the bed. He reached for it now, put it on, then opened his window and stepped out onto the side porch roof. Dropping lightly to the ground, he moved to the back alley, then darted to the rear of the nearest of the two empty adobe buildings.

Behind him he heard the riders stomping into the hotel's lobby. Bull was not very clever at his business. He should have sent riders to encircle the hotel before approaching it. The man was completely without stealth. No doubt in the past he had found no need for subterfuge of any sort. He had been able to rely on Jinglebob's enormous power and ruthlessness to gain whatever advantage he needed.

In a moment Bull and his riders would discover Longarm's absence and Red Notch would be overrun with anxious, gun-toting riders eager to do Harmon Dunstrom's bidding. Longarm was not sure if Dunstrom's purpose was to bring him in and hold him or to kill him outright. More likely it was the latter, judging from his selection of Bull Schofield as head of this posse. One thing was for sure, the owner of the Jinglebob was not about to give Longarm a chance to bring in the rest of the federal government, as Longarm had threatened to do.

Longarm had thrown down the gauntlet, and Harmon Dunstrom had wasted no time in snatching it up.

Longarm followed the alley behind the adobe building, then cut back to the main street. Peering around the corner, he watched the hotel entrance and was just in time to see the Jinglebob men spilling frantically out of the hotel and fanning out through the town. Three men darted into the alley in back of the hotel. Another jumped down from the side roof, just as Longarm had done a moment before. One man, sweating and puffing, his big Colt out and gleaming in the dark, ran down the street toward Longarm.

Longarm waited until the man was past him. Then he stepped out and flung his left arm around the man's neck. Yanking the fellow back into the shadows, Longarm kept enough pressure on his neck to prevent him from uttering a sound while he clubbed the man on the head as hard as he could. The man's struggling ceased and Longarm let him drop to the ground. Then, stepping out from behind the adobe, gun out like the rest of the Jinglebob crew, Longarm strode boldly toward the Jinglebob horses waiting in front of the hotel.

Mounting the nearest one, a powerful chestnut, Longarm yanked the horse back from the tie rack, and was clapping spurs to its flanks when someone cried out from behind him. By this time Longarm was at full gallop. Behind him came a flurry of shots followed by a chorus of furious, outraged shouts. Longarm kept going and almost at once he was in the hills.

Cutting off the trail, he rode with dangerous speed into the badlands, changing direction as often as he could. At last, finding a dark, lowering covey of boulders, he drifted in behind them, dismounted, and waited with his hand over the horse's snout. A storm of riders crested a ridge, then clattered past in the dark.

Longarm waited a decent interval, then mounted up, rode out from the rocks, and headed farther west. He had no intention of riding in the direction of the Wilk-

71

inson place. Those folks had enough trouble already.

About an hour later the moon rose, making it easier for Longarm to pick a trail through the hills. Soon he found himself once more in the sight of the river, descending to less hilly and rocky land. More than once he spooked small herds bedded down in tall grass. He was either approaching Jinglebob range, he realized, or that of one of the other big ranchers in the valley.

Before long, spread under the light of the moon, he saw a generous tangle of buildings ahead of him, the dark flank of a mountain at their back. If this was the Jinglebob, he told himself grimly, he would ask to see Jill Dunstrom and hope for the best.

He rode into the yard and headed for the main building, a long, low adobe and log affair. As he was dismounting someone flung open the front door and a woman stepped out, a rifle trained on him.

"Who in blazes are you, mister?" she demanded.

In the dim light, Longarm was not able to get a very clear picture of the woman's face. She was tall enough and big, but not outsized. From the sound of her voice he judged her to be in her early forties. She wore a broad-brimmed hat and had thrown a man's sheepskin jacket over her shoulders. Beneath the jacket he saw the long folds of a nightgown. She was standing in her slippers.

"Name's Long, Custis Long. I'm on the run from one of your neighbors."

"You mean Harmon Dunstrom?"

Longarm nodded.

"Stable your horse and get in here, then," she said.

"Thank you, ma'am."

72

"Don't stand around thanking me. Hurry up, so I can find a place to hide you."

Grinning, Longarm hurried toward the barn with his Jinglebob mount.

"We won't bother with lights," the woman said, holding the door open for him. "How far behind you are Jinglebob's riders?"

He turned to face her as she closed the door. It was still difficult for him to make out her features, but he could see that once they might have been considered handsome, if not pretty.

"I don't know for sure. I gave them the slip outside of Red Notch."

Longarm heard the scurry of light feet followed by an urgent knock on the door.

The woman turned. "Who is it?"

"Miss Compson! I just heard a rider come into the yard!" said a man's voice.

She pulled the door open. "I'm way ahead of you, Lash. He's on the run from Jinglebob. So you didn't hear nothing or see nothing. You got that?"

The old fellow nodded his head quickly as he peered past the woman in an effort to get a glimpse of Longarm. "Yes, ma'am. I got it, all right."

"Good night, Lash."

She closed the door and turned to Longarm. "In here. The fireplace is still going. That'll give us some light."

As he followed her into a large sitting room, he saw that she still held her rifle at the ready. He slumped wearily into a huge leather armchair and looked about him. In the dim, flickering light from the fireplace he became aware of trophies staring down at him from the wall and the careless, masculine clutter of chairs and sofas. The floor was covered by two large bearskins. He reckoned Miss Compson knew how to use the rifle she was carrying.

She sat down in a large wooden rocker across from Longarm and rested her rifle across the arms of it. "I'm Minnie Compson. This here's the Bar C. I run it myself since my Pa died three years ago. I ain't a widow; I just didn't find any men who wanted to marry me worth marrying."

Longarm smiled and withheld comment.

"Now suppose you tell me what you've done to put Harmon Dunstrom on your tail," she went on.

"I'm a deputy U. S. marshal, sent for by Sheriff Bingham. He figured this valley was about to explode and cabled for help. I've been riding through this country, sort of taking its measure. Not long ago, Dunstrom caught up with me in Red Notch and made me an offer. That was before he knew who I was and why I was here. When I refused, he rode out. Not long after his men arrived."

"What was his offer?" he asked.

"He wanted me to run for sheriff instead of Bull Schofield."

"That don't make no kind of sense."

Longarm explained briefly the events of that morning outside the restaurant in Harmony.

"So you licked the town bully, did you?" Minnie Compson said.

Longarm shrugged.

"And now Bull is out of favor with his boss, just

74

because he couldn't beat you to a pulp. Ain't that just like a man." She shook her head in mild disgust. "Maybe Tex Bingham should be replaced, cabling to the government for help like that. I figure if we can't handle the likes of Harmon Dunstrom without outside help, we deserve to lose this valley."

"I gather you don't think I should have been sent in here," Longarm said.

"You gather right, sonny."

Longarm grinned. "First time in a long time I been called that. I kind of like it. You must be over thirty-nine yourself, if I'm not mistaken."

"Not much over, Marshal. And I still got my needs, like any other healthy brute. But Harmon's our problem now, not my glands." She smiled suddenly. "Or yours."

Again Longarm felt it wise to withhold comment.

"How many are on your tail and how far back do you reckon they are?" she asked.

"At least six riders, but I'm pretty sure I lost them."

"Who was leading the pack?"

"Bull Schofield."

She nodded. "Looks like Harmon is giving the big ape a chance to redeem himself."

"That's about what I figured too."

"As you also probably figured by now, Bull ain't very smart, 'cept when it comes to trackin'. I figure that's because he's part animal. I wouldn't count on your losin' that bunch, not if Bull's leadin' them."

"I wouldn't have burst in on you like this if I hadn't thought there was little chance I'd be leading them to your place."

"You sure are full of chivalry, ain't you? Rolling in

the dirt to save Jill Dunstrom's honor and then gettin'
all discombobulated at the thought of Dunstrom's men
down on the head of this poor old woman."

"You do make me sound kind of silly, at that," Longarm said.

"I don't mean to poke fun at you, young man. It ain't
your fault you ain't dry behind the ears yet. But first
things first. I got a place to hide you, sure enough. It's
pretty damp down there, but you'll survive." She heaved
herself up out of her rocker. "Follow me."

The place Minnie Compson had in mind was her root
cellar. The way to it was through a doorway leading from
a broom closet. As Minnie lit a lamp and climbed down
ahead of him, she explained there was a time when the
root cellar had served as a hiding place from rampaging
Sioux. She left him with two quilted comforters filled
with chicken feathers and told him she would get him
up for breakfast. Then she climbed back up the narrow
wooden ladder and pulled the door shut behind her.

Longarm blew out the lamp she had left with him and
rolled up in the comforters. He found a sack of potatoes
to use as a pillow and tried to get comfortable. He felt
as if he were being put to bed without any supper for
being a bad boy.

Minnie Compson had that effect on people, he realized.

Chapter 5

Longarm awoke to the tramp of heavy boots on the floor above, and the unmistakable bark of Bull Schofield. Flinging off his comforter, Longarm unholstered his .44 and scrambled up the ladder. He pushed open the door inside the broom closet, then reached forward carefully and nudged the closet door open just a crack.

By that time it sounded as if a herd of buffalo had taken over the house. The walls resounded to the barks of excited men and the sound of furniture being dragged away from walls and lamps crashing to the floor. The Jinglebob riders were doing a thorough and determined job of searching the place, as if they were certain Longarm was on the premises.

And in that instant Longarm remembered the horse he had left in the barn. He had taken it from a Jinglebob rider. Undoubtedly it had a Jinglebob brand. Bull's men must have discovered it.

He heard Minnie Compson's furious, defiant responses to Bull's demands. She was admitting nothing beyond the fact that Longarm had stopped at her place the night before, borrowed a fresh mount from her, and continued on to Harmony. It sounded logical enough, but Bull wasn't buying.

Pulling himself up into the closet, he nudged the door open still wider and saw the back of Bull Schofield. The man's arms were akimbo, his hat riding on the back of his head, which was tipped ironically as he questioned Minnie. She was facing Longarm and had seen the door open a crack. With cold and deliberate calculation, she edged forward, causing Bull to take a step backward.

"...telling you, Minnie," Bull was saying. "There ain't no way you can weasel out of this. We found a Jinglebob horse in there, and not one of your mounts is missing. Every stall is full."

"That don't mean nothing, you jackass," Minnie countered. "I gave him a fresh horse from the pasture."

"In the middle of the night you went out there and roped a fresh mount for a stranger? You expect me to believe that?"

He was ready to hoot. A Jinglebob rider, a frown on his face, strode past them and out the door. As he left he told Bull he was going to check the barn again.

Longarm waited until this fellow left before pushing open the broom closet door and stepping lightly up behind Bull. The big man heard something and started to turn. Before he could, however, Longarm lifted his Colt out of its holster and brought the barrel down hard on the big man's skull. For a moment Longarm thought he was going to have to hit Bull a second time. Bull reared back, then began to grope like someone who had been struck blind before crumpling backward to the floor.

"Bull's a tough one, all right," Longarm commented, thrusting the Jinglebob foreman's Colt into his belt.

"Strong back, weak mind," Minnie said, glancing at him with some exasperation. "You're some lawman, you are, riding from Jinglebob riders on a Jinglebob horse, then leaving it in the barn."

"My apologies, Minnie."

She accepted Longarm's apology without comment, then glanced down at Bull's sprawled body. "Now what, Marshal?"

"Any Jinglebob riders still in the house?"

"Nope."

"Go to the door and call them back in. Tell them Bull wants them in here. See if you can make sure they come back in one by one."

"How do you suggest I do that?"

"Stand out there. Get in their way as they approach the door."

She shrugged. "I'll try it."

Minnie went to the door and stepped out. From the slant of the shadows, Longarm could tell it was still quite early in the morning. Bull Schofield had kept his men on Longarm's trail right through the night. He was sure as hell doing all he could to redeem himself in his boss's eyes.

Bull stirred. Longarm bent quickly and clipped him

on the skull again. Straightening up, he glanced at the Colt in his hand. He had the odd sensation he might have damaged it on Bull's head.

He heard Minnie calling the Jinglebob riders into the ranch house. Dragging Bull out of the kitchen, he hurried back into the room and took a position in front of the door. As the first Jinglebob rider entered, he found himself looking into the muzzle of Longarm's .44. Longarm put a finger to his mouth and motioned for the man to move to one side. In less than three minutes five Jinglebob riders were standing sheepishly in the kitchen, staring into the muzzle of Longarm's .44 and the Colt Longarm had taken from Bull.

"Disarm them, Minnie," Longarm told the woman as she came back into the kitchen.

With efficiency and despatch, Minnie did just that, tossing the weapons into the middle of the floor. "Now what?" she asked Longarm, when she was finished.

"Take one of those weapons and go in and keep a watch over Bull, while I go outside with these men. They have a long walk ahead of them and I want to be sure they get a good start."

As Minnie snatched up a revolver and hurried into the next room, Longarm smiled at the Jinglebob riders. "All right. Turn around and walk out of here. Any of you try anything and I'll send a round up your ass. There's no hurry. You got the whole day ahead of you."

Once outside, Longarm told the men to hold up and remove their boots. There was considerable grumbling about this, so Longarm sent a couple of rounds whistling past their feet. There was no more grumbling and the men began hopping frantically about as they pulled off their snug riding boots. By this time Lash and three more of Minnie Compson's hands had gathered to watch. Two of them looked as if they had been used rather roughly by some of the Jinglebob riders. They appeared to take a particularly grim delight in the sudden turnabout for Dunstrom's men.

Once the five men were in their stocking feet, Longarm said, "You men know which way Jinglebob is. Start walking."

The men had guessed what was ahead of them by this time. With more bitter grumbling, they turned and started walking. Grinning, Lash and the other Bar C hands watched them go.

"Make sure they keep going, Lash," Longarm told Minnie's foreman.

"You bet I will," Lash replied.

Returning to the house, Longarm found that Bull was conscious and had dragged himself up onto the leather sofa in Minnie's sitting room. He seemed to be having trouble focusing his eyes and was about as sociable as a treed bobcat. A thin trickle of blood from the spot where Longarm's blow had split his skull was running down across his forehead clear to his right eyebrow. The big man did not bother to wipe away the blood as he glared over at Minnie and Longarm. "You two are gonna regret this," he growled.

"Maybe," said Longarm. "But for now it is you and your riders who are going to regret coming in here like this. When you get back to Jinglebob, Bull, I want you to tell Harmon that this is not his valley. Tell him that there are more federal marshals where this one came from. I told him that not too long ago, but I reckon he wasn't listening. If he wants a war with these ranchers and farmers, he'll find himself fighting the U. S. government as well. He'll have a real tough time building that fancy slaughterhouse of his from a jail cell. Do you think you can remember all that, Bull?"

Bull just blinked and continued to glare.

Longarm waggled his gun. "All right. Your men have already left. It is only fair that you should join them. On such a long walk they'll need your encouragement."

Bull pushed himself to his feet. Longarm fell in behind him and kept his weapon trained on the foreman as he fumbled the door open and staggered out into the bright morning. The other Jinglebob riders were still in sight, straggling across the flat beyond the barn.

Longarm watched for a while as Bull stumbled after them. Then he turned about and went back into the ranch house. Minnie was at the stove, shoving in kindling. A fresh pot of coffee was sitting cold on top of the stove.

"What's all this about a slaughterhouse?" she asked, stepping back as the wood caught.

Longarm told her what Clyde Wilkinson had told him. She listened carefully. When he was finished, she frowned unhappily at him and shook her head.

"I remember that engineer fellow," she said, walking over to the table and slumping down into a chair. "I also remember I ain't seen him for a week now, and he used to find all kinds of excuses to stop by here for a cup of coffee and one or two of my fresh doughnuts. But he was always careful not to tell me what he was about."

"Maybe he should have stayed careful. Telling Wilkinson probably fixed his wagon for sure."

"I don't like it," she said, looking worried. "When it

82

was just greed on Harmon's part, we could deal with it. But this is more frightening. Harmon has been entertaining bigwigs from the railroad this past week. I know this for sure. If what you say is true, Harmon can't afford any more delays. He has got to get our land or he will lose out on this big scheme of his."

"Are there any other ranchers who have thrown in with him?"

Minnie shook her head. "No. He tried to buy out Ben Overmeyer of the Circle O and Nate Simpson of the Lazy S. They wouldn't sell, so he's fixed them real good."

"How so?"

"He's built a dam above their land, shutting off their only source of water. They've gone to court, but have lost each time. Jinglebob riders guard that dam around the clock. Ben and Nate are as angry as hornets, but what can they do against Jinglebob? Dunstrom's outfit has more riders than Ben and Nate combined."

"Who else opposes Dunstrom in this valley?"

"My spread and the Hammer, Pete Barry's horse ranch farther up in the hills on the other side of Red Notch. And Wilkinson." She cocked an eyebrow at Longarm. "Not a very impressive opposition, is it?"

"I wouldn't say that."

"Well, I would, and from what you've just told me, I think we're pretty close to being finished. Railroad money and influence is hard to beat."

"You don't think Dunstrom can be stopped?"

"How can he? After all, didn't he just send his bully boys after a federal marshal? And didn't they chase that federal marshal to my ranch and storm in here and tear this place apart to get him? That's what he thinks of the law, mister. Hell, he's owned the law in this valley so long, he thinks he *is* the law. And who knows? Maybe he's right."

"No, he is not right. There are laws, Minnie—even up here."

"Not for the likes of Harmon Dunstrom," she said wearily.

"You let me see about that," Longarm told her.

"All right, mister, I'll let you do that. But I hope the law doesn't arrive after we're all smoking ruin and ashes. It won't do us much good then."

The coffee pot began to perk. Minnie got up to tend to it, and Longarm took a deep breath. He had spoken with a hell of a lot more certainty than he felt.

It was close to sundown when Harmon Dunstrom rose suddenly to his feet, set down the drink his Indian housekeeper had just brought him, and shaded his eyes. Peering intently across the south flat, he was almost certain he saw six men on foot straggling toward the Jinglebob.

He was trying not to believe the evidence of his senses. But then Sam, his blacksmith, came running, with the cook right behind him, and he knew there was no way he could deny it. Bull and his men were returning on foot. Tim limped swiftly out of the horse barn, heading for the corral fence to get a better look. Harmon heard Jill's light footfall behind him as she stepped out onto the veranda.

"Harmon? Who are those men coming across the flat?" she asked.

"God damn it! How in blazes should I know?"

Jill laughed. It was a low, mean laugh that did not attempt to hide her malicious satisfaction. "Bull's been gone all day, hasn't he? And most of the men with him."

Harmon refused to reply to her. As Sam pulled up in front of the veranda to tell the boss what he already knew, Harmon cut him off brutally. "Never mind that! Go get Kelsey! Find him!" he shouted.

Meanwhile, Tim had turned and was limping swiftly back to the barn. Harmon knew instantly what the old wrangler intended. And he would not allow it. "Hold it right there, Tim!" he shouted. "Don't you bring out a single horse to those men. I want them to walk all the way, damn their hides!"

With a small, delighted laugh, Jill turned and hurried back into the house. Harmon had an idea where she was heading—to the balcony on the veranda roof. She would get a much better view of Jinglebob's footsore ranch hands from there, and she would like that.

Kelsey joined Harmon a few minutes later. He had some idea of his father's state of mind and said nothing. Harmon waited until the weary cowboys had almost reached the ranch before stepping off the veranda to intercept them.

"Stay with me, Kelsey," Harmon told his son. "And keep your mouth shut."

Pulling up a few feet from the gate, Dunstrom folded his arms and waited. The exhausted men would have to pass close by him on their way to the bunkhouse.

The first man to reach Harmon glanced bleakly at his boss. "We almost had him, Mr. Dunstrom. He—"

"I don't want to hear it, Tom! Just get out of my sight!" the boss ordered.

The next one started to explain also, but Dunstrom told him to keep on walking to the bunkhouse. The other men said nothing as they limped painfully past Dunstrom. Bull was still at least a hundred yards behind his men. Despite his enormous bulk and great strength, he appeared to be the most weary. Once or twice Dunstrom was certain the man was going to collapse. But he kept coming until at last he was standing before Dunstrom. Only then did Harmon see the smear of blood and dirt covering the big man's forehead. For just a moment the owner of the Jinglebob felt a faint glimmer of sympathy for his mountain of a foreman.

"Out with it, Bull! What the hell happened?" he demanded.

Bull licked his dry lips, panic brightening his eyes. "We almost had him, Mr. Dunstrom."

"Almost ain't good enough. Six men! I send six men in there to get him and you come back afoot."

"He gave us the slip at the hotel. But we tracked him all that night and picked up his trail at dawn. It led right to the Bar C."

"You mean he hid behind Minnie Compson's skirts?"

"That's right. We went in after him, but he came out of nowhere and slugged me. Then he got the drop on the rest of the men and made us all walk back."

"I gathered that. In short, he made fools of all of you. Wait until this gets around, Bull. You've really done yourself and Jinglebob proud. You'll make some sheriff, you will."

The big man appeared ready to cry.

"Go on! Get out of my sight!" Harmon Dunstrom snarled.

Bull started to move on past Harmon, then pulled up unhappily. "This fellow Long told me to tell you there's plenty more federal marshals where he came from. Is that what he is, Mr. Dunstrom, a federal marshal?"

"I said get on in there to the bunkhouse. Never mind what that son of a bitch told you. It ain't worth a pinch of coon shit!"

With a weary nod, Bull pushed on past Dunstrom. Whirling about, Dunstrom hurried back toward the ranch house with Kelsey at his side. Glancing up at the balcony, he saw Jill watching him. She still had that malicious grin on her face. He swore inwardly. How in the world could his brother have latched on to a bitch like that? he wondered.

"We got our work cut out for us, Kelsey," Dunstrom told his son. "And you're gonna have to do it without that big galoot to side you. Son, I want to know right here and now—can I count on you?"

"Sure, Pa," Kelsey said eagerly.

Dunstrom glanced at his son, at his pale gray eyes, his washed-out, narrow face framed by light, almost silken hair, and wondered for the hundredth time how this frail wisp of a man could have sprung from his loins. Well, maybe now was the time to see what Kelsey was made of. With Bull close to exhaustion, Dunstrom would have to rely entirely on his son. And maybe it was about time.

"Listen to me carefully, Kelsey," Dunstrom said as they reached the veranda. "I'm getting that loan I need in a couple of days. I am pretty damn sure I can buy off both the Lazy S and Ben Overmeyer with that money. Meanwhile, we can handle Pete Barry and Wilkinson without too much trouble. But I need time to set this up.

So I want you to see to it that Tex Bingham and this guy Long don't get a chance to wire for any more federal marshals."

"How could I do that, Pa?" Kelsey asked in bewilderment.

"God damn it! Use your imagination! Think!"

"You mean . . . !"

"I mean for you to do what you have to do to stop them from getting any more federal marshals up here. Cut the wires, why don't you? All I need is some time to pick up that loan and pay off Overmeyer and Simpson and buy that extra beef. The railroad will give us all we need then for the slaughterhouse. But I need time, son! Time!"

"Sure, Pa! Leave it to me."

"How soon can you pull out?" Dunstrom asked.

"Right now."

"No. Get something under your belt first."

"Oh, sure, Pa."

With a sigh, Dunstrom followed his son into the ranch house. He called to his housekeeper, and then started to make his own plans. While Kelsey was fixing that telegraph line, Dunstrom would have to tend to a few matters closer to home.

As Longarm loomed suddenly in his office doorway, Sheriff Bingham glanced up and smiled. The lawman was obviously pleased to see the federal man.

"Did you find out who shot Pedro and his woman?" he asked.

It was near sundown. Longarm had taken the long way back to Harmony, passing through Red Notch, where he had exchanged the Jinglebob mount he had borrowed for the dapple-gray. He would have to let Jinglebob know where they could pick up their horse. But that could wait. He had also stopped by Clyde Wilkinson's place to check on how Wilkinson and Kitty were doing.

Entering Bingham's office, Longarm said, "I don't have the slightest idea, Sheriff." He dropped wearily into the wooden chair by the desk.

"That's too bad," Bingham said. "Whoever did it was a crack shot. He could have cut us down, but he preferred to kill the Mexicans instead."

"I been thinking about that—among other things," Longarm said, "and I got this crazy idea it might have been Harmon Dunstrom."

"You're right. It *is* a crazy idea."

Longarm shrugged. "Let me tell you how crazy. I lost track of the rifleman, but not long after I realized I was being tailed. It was Dunstrom." Longarm grinned at Bingham. "That's right. Harmon Dunstrom. And when he caught up with me in Red Notch, he offered me your job as sheriff. Seems he's not so anxious to give it to his foreman, after all."

Bingham grinned. "Did you take him up on his offer?"

"Nope. After listening to what he had to tell me, I let the cat out of the bag. I told him who I was and why I was here."

Bingham frowned and leaned forward on his desk. "So what next?"

"I'm going to send my chief in Denver a wire. Tell him we need a few more federal marshals. With more badges to lean on, we shouldn't have too much trouble gathering a posse."

"I wouldn't count on that, if I were you."

"We'll see. But, first off, where's the nearest telegraph?"

"Center City, on the Northern Pacific line. It's about fifteen miles south of here. You want me to go with you?"

"No need for that. I'll leave first thing in the morning. Meanwhile, you might consider deputizing a few townsmen to help you keep order in the valley."

Bingham laughed bitterly. "There's not a townsman who would dare go against Dunstrom."

"I think you can change that," Longarm said.

"How?"

"Spread it around what Dunstrom is planning."

"And what, exactly, is he planning?"

Longarm told Bingham about the slaughterhouse Dunstrom was planning to build in Red Notch and how he was already deep in negotiations with the railroad. What that would do to the future of Harmony was obvious.

When Longarm finished, Bingham leaned back in his chair, thoughtful and impressed. "I see your point, Longarm. This could turn Harmony into a ghost town. We been hoping for a year now that we would get a spur in here to ship out the valley's cattle. After all, this is the county seat. Dunstrom's been talking it up for years."

"Not any more, he ain't. He'll be shipping out of Red Notch, the beef already dressed and ready for market."

"I'll let this news get out then. There's been talk about Red Notch, and all the digging and excavating going on there. But nobody knew what it was for and, besides, things had quieted down lately. The last time I rode by, all I could see was abandoned supplies and excavations, empty adobe houses, and a hotel nobody much was using."

"Red Notch will come alive as soon as Dunstrom closes the deal with the railroad. To do that, he has to have more land. So he's moving against the other ranchers. That dam he used to cut off the Circle O and the Lazy S is just the beginning."

"You go send that telegram and I'll spread the word, Long."

"Good. And it would not be a bad idea to get in touch with Overmeyer and Simpson. Send someone out to their places, or go yourself, first thing in the morning. Seems to me we should let them know they're not alone in their fight with Dunstrom."

Bingham nodded solemnly. "I'll see to it, Longarm."

"Good." Longarm sighed and got to his feet. "Now, how about joining me for a drink? I'm about as dry as a rattlesnake's belly. Besides, I've got a sack full of questions I want answered."

"I got no objections to that," the sheriff replied, getting to his feet also.

Taking out a cheroot, Longarm followed Bingham from his office. The last two days had been pretty crowded, and before he could see which way to go for sure, he would have to know more about the other ranchers opposing Harmon Dunstrom—Minnie Compson, especially.

So far, from what he could gather, she was one hell of a woman.

So pleased was Kelsey to be at last out from under the shadow of Bull Schofield, that he rode all that night.

If the sheriff or this new fellow planned to send a telegram, Kelsey knew, they would have to use the telegraph office in Center City. It was not yet dawn when he reached its outskirts. Looking down at it from a rise half a mile out, he saw that Center City was as still as the grave. He rode around the town and came in from the south, following the tracks. Dismounting a good distance from the depot building, he ground-reined his mount, then took off his spurs and walked the rest of the way to the telegraph office.

Before peering through the office window, Kelsey tied his bandanna over the lower portion of his face. A single lamp was glowing on the desk beside the telegrapher. Kelsey did not recognize the man. He was asleep with his feet up on the desk, his glasses pushed up onto his forehead, his long fingers clasped over his belly. With infinite care, Kelsey opened the outside door, then paused. The telegrapher did not stir. The sound of his snoring remained steady.

Opening the inner door, Kelsey approached the man from behind. He lifted his gun over his head and looked down at the man's unprotected skull. He was probably fifty years of age, Kelsey realized. For just an instant, the young man hesitated. Then he brought the gun barrel down with all the force he could muster, the way Bull would have done. The gun barrel caught the telegrapher on the forehead, over his left eye. The man was flung brutally from his chair by the force of the blow and lay on the floor unconscious—no longer snoring, as still as death. Kneeling by the old man's side, Kelsey felt his pulse. It was beating faintly but steadily.

Relieved, Kelsey stood up and ripped out the telegraph

key, stomped on it, then proceeded to pull out every other wire in the place. At last, surveying the wreckage with some satisfaction, he turned swiftly, let himself out of the place, and trotted to his horse through the cool morning air. Putting his spurs back on, he vaulted into the saddle and turned his horse south, following the tracks.

Five miles farther south, as the first faint rays of dawn fingered the eastern sky, Kelsey came to what he judged to be a good spot and dismounted. Here the wires passed so close to the canyon walls as to be almost lost in the rock's shadows. Peering up at them, he saw that unless he crowded in close behind the huge boulders and looked straight up, he would not be able to see the wires at all, so hidden were they by the canyon's gloom.

He checked to make sure he had everything he needed, then clambered up the rock wall until he was within reach of the wires. Swiftly he clipped them. The ends leaped apart. Climbing back down, he retrieved each end and made a tiny, barely visible loop. Then he took dark fishing tackle from his pocket, threaded it through the loops, and drew the wires together once again, until they were about a foot apart.

Holding the wires in his hand, he climbed back up and replaced them on the crossbars. Then he drew the tackle tighter, pulling the loops closer together until each end was less than a half inch from the other. Then he clipped off the excess tackle and crimped down the wires so that from the ground it would be almost impossible to see the tiny lengths of tackle that spanned the distance between the ends of the copper wires.

Once more on the ground, he peered up to inspect his handiwork. Unless he was looking directly at the spot where he had clipped the wires, he could not see what had been done.

Pleased, he mounted up and continued on down the track, this time keeping well out of sight of them as he rode. Later that morning, having passed another town that boasted a telegraph office, he veered back to the tracks and selected a spot where the wires had been strung through the branches of a thick stand of cottonwoods. Tying his horse up a short distance from the tracks, he climbed the trees and worked swiftly, doing an even better job this time.

After once more inspecting his handiwork, he hurried back to his horse, mounted up, and rode on south until he came to another isolated spot where the gleaming copper wires stood out clearly. Clambering up the pole, he boldly clipped the wires. This break they would find almost at once. It would satisfy the linemen until they resumed operations. Then would come the long, tedious search for the other breaks. They might find one of them in less than a week, but not both of them. At least this was Kelsey's hope. His father had asked for time. Well, he had given it to him—as much as he could.

With one last glance back at the downed copper strands gleaming in the bright sunlight, Kelsey mounted up and started back to the Jinglebob.

When Longarm reached Center City a little before noon earlier that same day, he found the place in an uproar. Someone had clubbed old Bill Finney, the telegrapher, to death and wrecked the telegraph office. Longarm was on his way to the train depot when he heard the talk.

He kept his mouth shut, entered the town's largest

saloon, and ordered a bottle of Maryland rye. Sitting in a corner, he listened as the townsmen filed in and discussed with an almost ghoulish relish the murder of old man Finney.

Finney had been found that morning lying on his side, facedown, the front of his forehead completely stove in directly over his left eye. It was, many said over and over, the most powerful, most brutal blow they had ever seen. Those who stole into the undertaker's parlor behind the barbershop to look for themselves came away shaking their heads at what they saw. And, as everyone in town knew by this time, Finney's wife was in the funeral parlor carrying on something awful and insisting on a closed coffin.

Longarm paid up and left Center City, heading for the next town down the line. He reached it by mid-afternoon and found that this line, too, was out of order. Messages could not be sent from the north, and nothing was coming from the south. There was some idle talk about Indian trouble, but no one really believed it. The wires were down, that was all. Western Union would get to it when it suited them. And only God knew when that would be.

Longarm turned back for Harmony. Dunstrom had sent someone to Center City and even farther south to prevent Longarm from cabling to Denver for more federal marshals. And there was little doubt in Longarm's mind which of his men he had sent.

Judging from the viciousness of that blow to the head of Bill Finney, it had to be Bull Schofield.

Chapter 6

Pete Barry, the owner of the horse ranch Minnie Compson had mentioned to Longarm, reined in his horse and cocked his head to listen. Had he just heard gunfire? After a few minutes, hearing nothing more, Pete nudged his horse forward. It must have been his imagination, he concluded.

A lean, rawboned fellow with thick red hair and a faint sprinkling of freckles over his youthful face, Pete was not the kind who expected, or looked for, trouble, though whenever it walked up to him, he had never willingly backed away. His pale green eyes seemed forever wide with expectation, his mouth always ready for a smile. Already there were laugh wrinkles around his eyes and mouth. He was a mustanger who loved his life, and everything about the young man broadcast this fact.

This bright morning he was returning from Beamer, a town close to the Canadian border. The Canadians were outfitting some kind of mounted police force to patrol the border and had become eager buyers for the mustangs Pete caught and broke. The old Frenchman who bought for the Canadians had given Pete good money for the bunch he had just driven up there and had kept the bargaining to a minimum—a clear indication to Pete that the Frenchman was able to sell the horses for a lot more than he was paying Pete.

But, hell, Pete was bringing home close to two thousand dollars, his best trip yet. His head bursting with plans, he was thinking now of turning a Percheron out with his best brood mares. The Frenchman had been asking about taller saddle horses and had indicated that a fine market awaited such mounts.

Topping a familiar rise, Pete pulled up and gazed down at the snug valley enclosing his small ranch. With great pride and affection, his eyes took in the single log cabin, the blacksmith shop, and the large horse barn. A tangle of corrals in excellent repair surrounded the compound. A swift, clean mountain stream ran behind the buildings and a stand of aspen served as an effective windbreak. Humble though his place was, Pete Barry was happy enough with it and pleased to be home again. He lifted his horse to a canter and swept on down the knoll toward the buildings.

As he rode into the yard, he saw his only hand, Tim Bronson, working with a bronc in the breaking corral. Nearly sixty years old, Tim had been a mustanger all his life and could still top a wild one. Riding up to the corral, Pete saw that Tim had the horse he was working, a blue roan stallion, gentled enough to rein to the right or left, with the animal bucking only once in a while—just to keep his hand in, so to speak.

"Hey, Tim!" Pete shouted from his saddle. His old partner was slightly hard of hearing. "Looks to me like you've got him gentled down."

Tim grinned at Pete. He had seen Pete coming, but had been too busy to let up. "All the fight ain't gone out of him yet. He still likes to bite and kick, and I have to tie him to the snubbing post to saddle him."

"Take a rest. I'll give the bastard a ride later."

Tim dismounted carefully. "Good to see you back."

"It's good to be back. Any excitement?" Pete asked.

Tim's eyes lit at once. "Know what I saw yesterday? That band of mustangs you been looking for, the one led by that big steeldust." Tim took his hat off and ran his hand through his thick shock of snow-white hair. "There's a lot of good horseflesh in that bronco's band, I tell you."

"Maybe we should go after him again," said Pete. "I'm willin'. Think you could keep up?"

"Try me!" the old man shouted gleefully.

"Soon as I get a chance to rest these bones."

Tim's long, wrinkled face got serious all of a sudden. "How was the trip?" he asked, opening the corral gate and leaving the corral.

Pete patted his money belt. "We're both of us rich as sin, Tim. Real plutocrats. I got some plans I'd like to talk over with you."

"I'll put some fresh coffee on," Tim said, starting for the ranch house. "Tend to your horse and join me inside."

Pete nodded and turned his horse back toward the barn. As he did so, he let his gaze sweep the flat below his ranch. Halfway to the barn, he frowned and pulled up. His gaze had caught something he didn't like crouched or sitting in the deep grass. It was too large for a deer, and it didn't have the look of a beef cow. But it was an animal of some kind, easily as big as a horse. But it wasn't moving. Pete glanced skyward. A buzzard was circling in the high blue morning sky.

Tim had disappeared into the ranch house by this time. Deciding against calling Tim back, Pete spurred his horse out of the yard and cantered onto the flat, heading straight for the downed animal—for that was what it was, he knew now for certain. As he reached it and flung himself from his saddle, a groan escaped his lips.

It was one of his best mares. He looked with horror at her unblinking, staring eyes. Next he saw the flies, his gaze following them to the bullet hole behind the mare's ear. He stood up, looking wildly about him, his heart pounding painfully in his throat. He was remembering those shots he had heard earlier. It was easy to understand why Tim had not heard them. The old man was hard of hearing to begin with, and above his own shouts and the pounding hooves of that roan he was breaking, there had been practically no chance at all he would have heard anything.

But who would do such a thing? And why? Pete thought wildly. And what of his other horses?

Catching at his mount's rein, he swung into the saddle and spurred wildly on past the stand of cottonwoods, sweeping into the broadest portion of his valley. He had constructed a long pole fence at its far end to keep his stock securely penned. Sweeping down through the center of the valley, he soon came in sight of the fence. He kept riding and it was not long before he saw the other dead horses, their carcasses obscene stains on the lush grass. Again he glanced up. The sky was filling with buzzards circling cautiously, monstrous cinders hovering in a hellish updraft.

He didn't ride any further. His heart pounding with rage, he pulled up, wheeled his horse around, and started back for the ranch. That was when he saw them: the large herd of cattle spilling down out of the breaks into the valley. Jinglebob riders were hazing them, their shrill whistles piercing the morning stillness. They must have been watching him, waiting until he had ridden on past them before releasing the cattle down into the valley.

The foreman directing the operation from a small hillock was recognized instantly by Pete. It was Bull Schofield.

Pete clawed the sixgun from his holster and spurred directly for the big foreman. Bull sat his horse heavily, impassively, his mouth a straight line of cruel indifference. When Pete came within a couple of hundred yards, Bull snaked his Winchester out of his saddle sling. Pete saw the Jinglebob foreman lever a fresh cartridge into its firing chamber. Out of the corner of his eyes, he saw two Jinglebob riders galloping down toward him from the slope on his left.

Ignoring them, Pete fired at Bull. But Pete had never been a good shot. Though his round came close enough to cause Bull's horse to shy nervously and lift its head, it went on past Bull. Quieting his mount with a single sharp command, Bull brought up his rifle and sighted carefully along the barrel. Again Pete fired. This second round was just as fruitless. He saw Bull's mouth crease into a mean grin as he squeezed off his first shot.

Pete heard the bullet's impact as it plowed into his horse's chest. As if all four of his feet had been sliced off at the knees, the animal plunged to the ground, throwing Pete over his head. Pete struck the thick grass lightly, kept tumbling, and vaulted to his feet, his sixgun still in his hand.

Before he could raise it to fire, however, the two Jinglebob riders flung themselves on Pete. One of them wrested Pete's sixgun from his hand while the other pinned his arms behind him. Bull dismounted and walked toward Pete. He came to a halt a foot from the young mustanger and punched him in the mouth. Pete felt his head snap back and, before he could straighten up, Bull drove another brutal punch into his gut. Doubling over, Pete vomited. Another blow stung his head behind his ear and he felt himself strike the ground. Pulling himself into a protective ball, he hung on as Bull began kicking him about the head and shoulders in a furious effort to get his boot in past his guard.

At last, his rage having exhausted him, Bull stepped back and glanced at one of his men. "Get him up," he wheezed, breathing heavily.

Pete felt himself hauled upright. He had a difficult time staying on his feet. His vision of Bull was marred by a thin, bloody veil that insisted on sluicing down across his eyes. When he tried to wipe it away, he found his arm felt as heavy as an anvil. The blood pouring from one nostril tasted sweet. He licked at it to keep his mouth open so he could breathe.

"You better kill me now, Bull," Pete told the Jinglebob foreman, "because if you don't, I'll kill you first chance I get."

The man standing beside him struck him on the side of his head with the barrel of his revolver. The next thing Pete knew he was sprawled full length on the blood-slick grass, trying with no success to pull himself upright. All he could manage was to turn about and stare dazedly up at Bull.

"Do that again, Ned," the furious foreman told the hand, "and I'll club you silly. We got to keep this guy alive long enough to get his signature, damn it! Now haul him back up."

Again Pete found himself facing Bull. The universe was tipping wildly under him and he kept telling himself this was all some crazy dream, that he was back in Beamer selling his horses to that Frenchman. He shook his head and found when he did that it became so painful he almost lost consciousness. As he sagged, hands reached out quickly to steady him.

"See what you done, Ned, for Christ's sake!" Bull snarled at his man. "Now don't you let him fall again."

Pete heard Ned's grudging response. Then Bull stepped closer, peering at Pete carefully as he did so. There was a pencil and a paper in the foreman's hand.

"Here you go, Pete," Bull said, as if he were talking to the village idiot. "See this here piece of paper? All you have to do is sign it and we'll leave you be."

"What is it?" Pete managed.

"It's a bill of sale. Mr. Dunstrom's giving you a thousand dollars for this here ranch and valley. He's being very generous. He owns the hills above you. He could just dam the stream if he wanted, like he does to Ben Overmeyer and Nate Simpson. Sign this and take the money."

"I ain't signing nothin'."

Pete waited for Bull to step back and slap him around some more. But Bull just straightened carefully and studied Pete's battered face for a moment. Pete could see how difficult it was for Bull to think his way through this one. Then Bull licked his lips and smiled. "We could beat you some more. We could *make* you sign, Pete. You know we could do that."

"You got some Apache blood in you. That it, Bull?" Pete asked.

Forgetting himself, Bull slapped Pete hard. For a moment Pete thought he was going down a third time, but the two hands hung on to him and kept him upright.

Pete managed a smile. "Do your worse, Bull, but I ain't signin' that bill of sale, and I ain't takin' any of your blood money."

Bull took a deep breath and stepped back. "I guess maybe you ain't, at that. Not for your own self, that is." He grinned at his two hands then. "Haul him up to his ranch house," he told them.

When they reached the ranch house, Pete saw that two other Jinglebob hands had Tim Bronson in their custody. Tim was standing beside the door, the men close at his side. There was a mean cut over Tim's right eye. When Pete got closer and Tim saw Pete's condition more clearly, he tried to break away from the two men to hurry to Pete's side. But one of the men slapped the old man hard on the side of the head, knocking him back against the ranch house wall.

"Get him inside!" barked Bull.

The men hauled Tim into the cabin and a moment later Pete followed him inside. The place was a shambles, testifying to the struggle Tim must have put up when he was surprised by the Jinglebob riders. The table and chairs were overturned. The coffeepot Tim had been filling lay in a corner, the coffee grounds spread over the floor.

"Sit the old son of a bitch at the table," Bull said.

One of the men righted a chair and shoved Tim down into it. Another Jinglebob hand picked up the table and shoved it against Tim, then stood back. Bull moved closer to Tim and looked down at the old man. "Howdy, Tim," he said.

Tim said nothing.

Bull smiled. "I guess you think you're a tough old son of a bitch, don't you?"

Tim looked up, cleared his throat, and spat full in Bull's face.

Bull leaped back, swiping wildly at his face. Then he roared back at Tim and with one violent punch sent the old man flying from the chair. At once Pete tried to break free and go to Tim's aid. But the two men holding onto Pete kept both his arms twisted up behind him, rendering him immobile.

Bull's punishment was swift and lethal. After a few brutal, measured blows to Tim's frail body, Tim was hauled back up onto the chair and held there by one of Bull's men.

His face still flaming with rage, Bull spun on Pete. "I've had it with you two," he snarled heavily. "Harmon told me to go easy, but I don't have to if I don't want to. And right now I'd like nothing better than to wipe the floor of this place with both of you. Now, you going to sign this bill of sale?"

Defiantly, Pete shook his head.

Bull swung back to Tim and grabbed the old man's right wrist. Forcing his hand out straight on the table, Bull lifted his sixgun from its holster, flipped it so the butt was facing down, then brought the gun butt down as hard as he could on the knuckles of Tim's hand. The man cried out in agony, then peered through streaming eyes at his ruined hand. Desperately, he tried to pull his hand back. Bull squared his shoulders, raised his gun butt a second time, and brought it down once again upon Tim's twisting, shattered hand.

Tim let out one terrible cry, then dropped his head and sagged forward onto the table, unconscious.

Bull looked back at Pete. Pete could feel the tears crowding his eyes—tears of rage and hopelessness.

"Damn you, Bull, oh, damn you to hell!"

Bull grinned. "You want me to ruin this old fool's other hand, do you? He's out completely now and won't feel a thing. Not till he wakes up, that is."

"You son of a bitch."

Bull walked over to Pete and punched him in the stomach hard. As Pete doubled over, Bull grabbed a fistful of Pete's hair and hauled his head up. "Don't you ever call me a son of a bitch again, Pete," he said softly, "or I'll kill you."

His hand still in Pete's hair, he dragged him over to

106

the table and slapped the bill of sale down onto it. Fishing in his jacket for a pencil, he thrust it at Pete. Pete took it. It was difficult for him to focus his eyes to find the place to sign. When Bull saw his difficulty, he rested his forefinger on the spot.

"Sign there," he said, "or I'll start on Tim's other hand."

Pete signed.

Bull snatched up the bill of sale and the pencil. Then he took a thick envelope out of the inside pocket of his sheepskin and flung it down onto the table. "There's your money. You got until tonight to clear out. If we find you here tomorrow morning, we'll likely kill you both for trespassing."

With a sharp nod to his men, he herded them out the door ahead of him. Slumping down beside Tim at the table, Pete Barry did not even look up as Bull and the rest of the Jinglebob riders mounted up and rode off.

Harmon Dunstrom, sided by only a single Jinglebob rider, had left Pete Barry's Hammer ranch to his foreman because he did not trust Bull to handle this business with Wilkinson with the delicacy that was required.

Not that Harmon felt anything but contempt for that mealymouthed lawyer. It was Wilkinson's daughter, Kitty, who generated Harmon's concern. He liked the girl's gumption—and a lot more besides. He was sure that once he had weaned her from that sniveling old man of hers, there would be no reason why he could not show her how a real ranch is run.

Hell, if things went the way they should this morning, he just might invite the two of them to stay at the Jinglebob as his guests. He knew such a circumstance would drive that bitch Jill up one wall and down the other, but that was no concern of his. The important thing was that once he gained Kitty's undivided attention in this fashion, he was almost certain he would have little difficulty in pointing out to her what advantages and even luxuries he could provide as her husband.

Surely after what she must have gone through these past three years, attempting to make profitable her father's wretched ranch, she should be more than willing to listen to Harmon's proposal. The trick, therefore, would be to gain her father's holdings as pleasantly and as painlessly as possible so that there would be no residue of unpleasantness for him to cope with during his courtship. Accordingly, he was riding up this day with what he knew to be a magnanimous offer of two thousand dollars.

And that for Wilkinson's entire holdings, even though Harmon was well aware that the man had paid less than eight hundred dollars for the entire ranch to begin with, when at the time it was stocked with superb beef and the buildings were in far better repair than they were at present. And this generosity was in the face of the damage the puny little worm had already done to his cause by blabbing to everyone in earshot about Harmon's plans for Red Notch.

Harmon Dunstrom was well pleased with himself. It wasn't often he could be talked into doing the right thing for no reason other than that it was simply the right thing to do.

Topping a rise, he got an uninterrupted glimpse of Wilkinson's ranch, and almost immediately his disgust at the way Wilkinson had allowed the place to run down began to get the better of him. What a pitiable excuse for a ranch this place had become, he realized. The poor little son of a bitch hadn't even settled on a name for it yet. He didn't even have a brand registered. Harmon shook his head as he realized how many of the lunger's cattle had already wandered away and got lost in the breaks above this place, or been roped and branded as mavericks by the Lazy S or the Circle O.

Well, it didn't really matter all that much, he told himself. It would all come back to the same destination in the end: his slaughterhouse.

He pushed past the half-open gate, his rider pulling up and trailing behind him. Glancing back at the hand, Harmon said, "Don't say anything, Lem. Just let me do the talking. This won't take long."

Lem nodded.

Harmon turned back around and rode into the small compound. When his eyes caught sight of the rusted cultivator abandoned in the front yard, he shook his head slightly in disgust. He pulled up and started to dismount.

Kitty Wilkinson appeared in the doorway, a big Winchester in her hands. "Hold it right there, Harmon!" she told him. "You hit that ground and you're a dead man. No one asked you to light and set."

"Well, now," he told her, "I'm half on and half off. Why not let me get all the way down, Kitty? I ain't come here to cause trouble."

"Get back up on that horse, then." This time it was Clyde Wilkinson speaking. He had come out from behind the barn, and he also held a rifle in his hands.

Harmon swung his right leg over the cantle and settled

his huge frame back into the saddle. It squeaked under his considerable heft. He swallowed and took a deep breath. This was not going at all the way he had planned.

"This ain't very neighborly," he told the Wilkinsons.

"You ain't much of a neighbor," Wilkinson snapped.

"Well, I aim to change that."

"Do you, now?" the sick man sneered.

The little fool walked closer, the rifle trained on Harmon. The fellow was so thin and wispy he resembled a scarecrow run off from some cornfield. Harmon did not like such a frail creature aiming a Winchester at him. The poor little son of a bitch could easily trip over something and loose a round at Dunstrom without even meaning to do so.

"Damn it, Wilkinson," Harmon protested, "put down that rifle! I told you, I came here to talk reasonable."

"Like civilized men, you mean."

"That's it. Of course."

Wilkinson smiled and turned to look at his daughter. "What do you think, Kitty? Can we trust the son of a bitch?"

"No!" Kitty snapped.

A malicious gleam in his eye, Wilkinson looked back up at Harmon. "She's right, Harmon. I never go wrong taking her advice. State your business, then ride out of here."

Harmon was outraged. But one glance at the way Kitty Wilkinson stood in the doorway and he knew he could not allow himself to get all hot and bothered. Swallowing his pride, he said, "I've come to make an offer for your place, Wilkinson. And I consider it a fair and generous one. Now, if you would do me the kindness to let me light and set, we can discuss this like civilized people."

Kitty stepped out of the ranch house doorway then and walked closer to Harmon. She was a fine slip of a woman, and that was a fact.

"We don't want to sell, Mr. Dunstrom," she told him flatly.

"Now, Kitty," her father said, "let's hear the man out before making any rash statements."

"Fair enough," Harmon said, resigned finally to conducting this entire negotiation from the back of his horse. "For this ranch," he began impressively, "I am willing to offer you—in cash—two thousand dollars."

"In cash," Wilkinson repeated.

Harmon nodded emphatically. "Yes, in cash. I have it with me now."

"Pretty sure of yourself, aren't you?" said Kitty.

"I think it is a fine offer," Harmon replied.

"And we would be fools to refuse it?" she asked.

"I did not say that," he told her carefully.

Kitty looked at her father. Wilkinson cleared his throat. "You're about ready to build that slaughterhouse, I suppose," he said to Harmon.

"Yes, I am."

"So you'll need this land. That flat along the river, anyway. Not to mention all that fresh water."

Dunstrom shifted uncomfortably in his saddle. Damned if he liked this inquisition, especially from the likes of this old fool. "You know all that is perfectly true, Wilkinson," he replied testily. "So what are you trying to say?"

"That two thousand dollars is a paltry sum for this land. Never mind the buildings and the stock."

That did it. Dunstrom felt all self-control slip away from him. "You're goddamn right!" he cried. "Never mind the buildings and the stock. You've let the buildings rot and your stock is halfway to hell and gone. You're a hopeless incompetent as a rancher, Wilkinson, and here I am offering to bail you out. You ought to get down on your hands and knees and thank God there's someone in this county with gumption enough to build that slaughterhouse. Who else would be fool enough to give you cold cash for this disaster you call a ranch?"

Wilkinson pulled up and smiled somewhat feebly at the rancher. "I guess maybe you've got a point there, Dunstrom. I been feeling poorly since I got here, and this damned climate ain't done what I thought it would for me. So you're right. As a rancher, I leave much to be desired."

"Then take my offer!" Dunstrom insisted.

"No."

"Damn it! Why not?"

"I'm stubborn, I guess. I don't like you, and I don't like what you've already done to get that blamed slaughterhouse into operation. So the answer is no. And don't bother to argue or raise the ante. I'm not selling."

Dunstrom swung around to look at the girl. She was beaming.

"You'll regret this," Dunstrom told them.

"You're threatening us, are you?" Kitty asked.

"That's the only language fools like you will ever understand."

Kitty stepped forward and fired her rifle into the air. It went off inches from Dunstrom's horse. Rearing in panic, the horse flung Dunstrom from his saddle. As he tumbled to the ground, he pulled the animal down with him. Taking a quick step forward, Wilkinson kept his rifle trained on the other Jinglebob rider. Searing the air with curses, Dunstrom pulled himself free of his horse, yanked it furiously back up, and remounted.

"You asked for it," he snarled at Kitty, wheeling his horse about. "And you'll get it."

"Get off my land or the next bullet will ream your ass!" Wilkinson snarled.

Spurring his mount ahead of his ranch hand, Dunstrom rode out of the yard. When he reached the sagging gate, he grabbed it furiously and pulled it from its remaining hinge. A rifle shot cracked behind him and he felt his hat go flying. Unholstering his sixgun, Dunstrom spurred his horse to a boulder, dismounted, and turned to face the ranch. As he did so, he saw Kitty and her father duck inside the cabin. That suited Dunstrom just fine. Lem pulled up beside him and looked down in some confusion. Dunstrom glared up at him.

"Damn it, Lem!" he cried. "Get off that horse and give me a hand. We're going to blast them out of that flea trap before nightfall. Then we're going to burn it to the ground. And we ain't gonna pay them a cent. Now get off that horse and move around behind the barn."

"What do you want me to do when I get there?" Lem asked.

"Pour lead into that place until it smokes. I'll tell you when to stop!"

"We might kill them."

"Keep your shots high. Break all their windows.

They'll be on the floor, praying. When it gets too hot for them, they'll quit and come out. Then we'll go in and torch the place."

"Boss, are you sure—"

"Damn it to hell, Lem. Do what I tell you!"

Nodding unhappily, Lem dragged his carbine out of his saddle sling and vanished behind the boulder, on his way to the other side of the barn. Harmon took his own rifle out and trained it on the door. He sent two quick rounds into it and saw it splinter. Then, from the window beside it, a rifle barrel was poked out. It spat fire and a round ricocheted off the ledge over his head. The bullet had come uncomfortably close, and Harmon hunched down, seething in frustration.

But once Lem began his fusillade, Dunstrom moved out from behind the boulder and found a better vantage spot closer to the cabin. He then began to fire back through the window and soon had them all free of glass. Fire from the cabin came only sporadically, and after a while Dunstrom held up.

"All right, Lem!" he called over to the barn. "Hold off a minute!"

Lem stopped firing. The sudden silence was oppressive. Peering out from around the boulder he had been using for cover, Harmon saw no sign of life from within the cabin. He aimed his rifle at the heavens and fired. The shot echoed and reechoed, but there was no response from the cabin. Dunstrom remembered Lem's earlier fear and began to wonder if he might have gone too far. It sure as hell would not look good if any harm came to that girl because of him.

He stood up and stepped out from behind the boulder.

If they were in there waiting for their chance, this was it. But still nothing came from the cabin, no sound, no answering shot, no cry of defiance. Panic stirred within Harmon and he took a step closer. When still there was no sign of life, he kept coming. Lem too left the cover of the barn and joined him. Soon, both were running toward the cabin.

Less than ten yards from it, the splintered door was flung open. Kitty and her father crowded out, pouring shots into the ground at Harmon's and Lem's feet. Both men hauled up and started dancing.

"Stop it!" Harmon cried. "Stop it! You're liable to hurt us!"

"Drop your guns, then your pants—both of you!" Wilkinson cried.

Harmon dropped his rifle and began fumbling with his belt. He moved as fast as he could, but Lem got his pants off first.

"Now turn around," Kitty said, "and ride on out of here. Both of you!"

Harmon wore red longjohns, and one rear button was missing. He could feel the flap slapping at his thigh as he ran. It made him want to reach back and cover his ass, but he was too anxious to get away. He flung himself hastily into his saddle, yanked his mount around, and beat Lem over the rise.

A few miles later, he pulled up and waited for Lem to reach him.

"Lem," he said, "if you mention this to *anyone* you're fired."

"Sure, boss. But how we gonna explain we ain't got our britches on?"

"We ain't. We'll ride in late."

"Sure, boss."

Dunstrom nudged his horse on and glanced at the sun. There was still a couple of hours of daylight left. So they would just have to ride slower. And, next time, he would send Bull Schofield.

Chapter 7

As Longarm rode up to the hitch rack in front of the sheriff's office late that same day, Bingham stepped out onto the boardwalk and watched him dismount, a troubled, bemused look was on his face.

"You look like you need something to wash down that dust," the sheriff said.

Longarm nodded, loosened the cinch strap, and took off his hat. After slapping it against his thigh to scare off the dust, he clapped it back on, then brushed off his arms and the front of his jacket. Then he met Bingham's gaze.

"That's about what I need, all right. Lead the way."

The two men strode down the street to the Cattleman's Rest. Spotting a table in back, they plowed through the sawdust to it. As they settled in their chairs, Bingham called over to the barkeep for a bottle of rye. When it came, the sheriff poured.

Longarm tossed the rye down. It warmed him considerably.

"You go first," Bingham said.

"You look anxious, Sheriff. Maybe you got some news, too."

"I sure as hell have. Fortify yourself again and tell me what you've got. After that, I'll tell you what's been happening around here. Then I suggest we take a walk so I can show you."

Longarm poured himself another belt, downed it, then broke out a cheroot. Handing one to the sheriff, he lit his own and then Bingham's with a sulfur match.

"I didn't send any telegram," he told the sheriff.

"Why not?"

"The telegrapher at Center City was dead when I got there. Clubbed to death. And the lines were cut well past the next town. It'll take a while before they find all the breaks, I'm thinking."

Bingham frowned. "My God," he whispered, "murdered? That's terrible. I guess that explains it, then. Harmon Dunstrom has let his dogs loose."

Longarm nodded gloomily. "That's about what I figured, too. But murdering that poor old son of a bitch in Center City is an indictable offense. I'm itching to get the bastard responsible. And I got just the right candidate."

"You're thinking Bull Schofield."

"You're damned right I am. It had the look of him, I'm telling you. A brutal, crushing blow to the forehead

118

with a gun butt or barrel. All I'd need is a witness placing him in the vicinity."

Bingham shook his head unhappily. "Afraid you're not going to get that."

"What do you mean?" Longarm asked.

"That son of a bitch has been too damn busy up here."

Longarm cocked an eye at the sheriff. "All right, then. It's your turn. Let's hear what you got."

"Bull and a few other Jinglebob riders visited Pete Barry's Hammer ranch this morning. Seems Harmon wanted Pete to sign a bill of sale. Bull had it all ready for Pete's signature, plus one thousand in cash. Pete refused, so Bull went to work on him. But that got him nowhere, so he turned his attention to Pete's ranch hand, an old stove-up cowpoke name of Tim Bronson. Right now the doc is trying to fix Tim's right hand, but he thinks he might have to take it off."

Longarm leaned back in his chair and chucked his hat back off his forehead. "Jesus."

"And you should see what Pete looks like. One more thing: while they were at it, Bull and his boys shot all of Pete's horses."

"Did Pete sign the bill of sale?"

"What would you have done?" the sheriff asked bitterly. "Bull was anxious to begin on Tim's other hand."

"And did he take the money?" Longarm asked.

Bingham nodded. "He did. Right now, it's tucked away in my office. He gave it to me for safekeeping. Evidence, he calls it."

"You mean he's pressing charges?"

"That's exactly what I mean."

"He's signed a complaint?" Longarm was astonished.

"He has."

"And you have a warrant," Longarm said.

Sheriff Bingham tapped his breast pocket and smiled ruefully. "Now you know how much I wish you had been able to telegraph Denver. We could use those extra federal marshals."

"How about scaring up a posse?"

Bingham laughed. "Scaring is the right word. But no one in town is scared enough to go after that crew."

"You spread the word, like I told you?"

"About what Dunstrom is planning for Red Notch?"

"That's right."

"Sure, I did. A few eyebrows went up and one or two merchants swore bitterly. A few even stopped what they were doing and stomped in here to discuss it with other merchants. That was about the size of it."

Hearing this, Longarm wondered why he was surprised. If these people hadn't stood up to Harmon Dunstrom before, there was no reason to believe they would begin now. After a while doormats had no trouble lying flat.

"Well, then," he said, "what about Overmeyer and Simpson?"

"I sent a note out to both of them after you left this morning. So far I ain't heard nothing. The rider I sent hasn't even got back yet."

"Who'd you send?"

"A kid hangs around the livery stable. He's trustworthy, Longarm, and a good rider."

Longarm sighed. "So, for now, that leaves it up to

us." He poured himself one more drink, stoppered the bottle, then downed the rye. "Let's go," he said. "I want to talk to Pete Barry."

"Thought you would."

"He's mad now," Longarm said, getting to his feet. "But what we got to worry about is, will he still be as anxious to testify when the time comes? Especially if Dunstrom comes up with more cash to sweeten the deal."

"I don't think we have to worry about that, Longarm."

Leading the way out of the Cattleman's Rest, Longarm glanced back at the sheriff. "I hope you're right," he said.

In his office above the barbershop, Dr. Avery Pendelton turned as Longarm and Sheriff Bingham entered. A lean, cadaverous fellow with gray chin whiskers and no hair to speak of on his bald pate, he frowned through steel-rimmed spectacles at them and straightened. Striding in from the outer office, Longarm looked past the doctor at the old cowpoke who lay unconscious on a cot against the wall.

Tim Bronson's right hand was covered by a bloody cloth. A strong, powerful odor came from a carbolic mixture sitting in a basin on a table by the cot. Wrapped in a bloody towel beside the basin was a gleaming set of cutting instruments. Longarm glimpsed one saw-toothed edge sticking out of the far end of the towel. The edge was not clean.

"How is he, doc?" he asked.

"You the federal marshal?" Pendelton asked.

"That's right."

"Where the hell were you when this was going on?"

"About thirty or so miles south of here, looking for a place to send a telegram."

"Well, you should have been up here." The doctor looked past Longarm at Bingham. "There's no excuse for you either, Sheriff. You've known all along what an animal Bull Schofield is."

Sheriff Bingham nodded unhappily.

"I'm still waiting for your answer," Longarm snapped. "How is he?"

"As well as can be expected," the doctor snapped back.

Waving them out angrily, he walked toward them. Longarm backed up hastily, and Bingham did as well. As soon as they had been chased back to the doctor's outer office, the doctor reached swiftly for the doorknob and closed it in their faces, then shot the bolt.

"He's a real sweetheart, that one," commented Longarm.

"He's a good doctor, though. He never amputates unless he has to, and when he does, he uses that chloroform stuff."

"That makes me feel much better," said Longarm.

The door behind them opened. Longarm turned to see a young man limp into the office. Had it not been so fearfully battered and swollen, his would have been a cheerful, freckled face, one that radiated optimism. Not now, however.

Frowning, the fellow paused when he saw the two of them standing there.

"Longarm," Bingham said quickly, "this here is Pctc

Barry. Pete, meet Custis Long. He's a deputy U. S. marshal."

Pete shook Longarm's hand. "You going to go after Bull, Deputy?"

"That's right."

"When you do, I want to go along."

"You just stay back here and look after Tim," Sheriff Bingham said. "Longarm and I don't need your help. You ain't in any proper condition to give it, either. Not after what you been through."

"I can still ride and I can still pack a gun. You ain't going to stop me, Sheriff. I'll go with you two or I'll go alone."

"You're welcome to come with us, Pete," said Longarm. "Just remember you'll be part of a lawful delegation. There won't be any gunslinging if I can help it."

Pete nodded grimly. "All right, you have my word."

"That's good enough for me."

The door behind them opened up. The doctor stood in the doorway. He ignored Longarm and the sheriff and looked at Pete. "You better get in here, Pete."

Pete brushed hurriedly past Longarm and into the office. The doctor closed the door quickly behind him. Longarm looked at Bingham, who shrugged, turned, and led the way out of the office.

They were sitting in the sheriff's office making plans for the next day's ride to the Jinglebob spread when they heard the sudden screaming. It was a soul in such torment it made their skin crawl. Both men jumped to their feet and rushed out into the night. The cries were coming

123

from the room over the barbershop—Pendelton's office. As suddenly as they hàd begun, the screams stopped. Longarm looked around and saw others who, like he and Bingham, had rushed out into the night when the screaming began.

Longarm followed the sheriff back inside his office and slumped wearily into the chair beside Bingham's desk. The sheriff hauled out his bottle and two glasses and poured stiff belts for each of them.

"The doctor had to amputate, seems like," said Bingham, replacing the bottle.

"I thought you said the doc uses chloroform."

"He does."

"That sure as hell didn't sound like it."

Pete Barry appeared in the doorway, eyes stricken, his face the color of a bedsheet. "The doc took off Tim's hand," he said.

"We heard," said Longarm. "What happened? Didn't the doc use anything to kill the pain?"

"He was all out of chloroform, and he didn't have any whiskey handy."

Longarm looked at the sheriff. This Pendelton was some doctor, all right.

"I got something for what ails you right here," Bingham said, lifting the bottle of whiskey.

"I don't want nothing to drink, Sheriff. I just want to ride out to the Jinglebob tomorrow and help you bring in Bull. He should have to go to prison for this—and for a good long time."

"Not long enough, though, Pete," said the sheriff.

"But he will do time," Longarm said, "that's for damn sure."

Pete smiled thinly. "Maybe he won't go quietly."

"Where are you staying, Pete?" asked the sheriff.

"At the hotel."

"We'll be pulling out at dawn."

Pete nodded and vanished from the doorway. Sheriff Bingham looked over at Longarm and shook his head wearily.

"I think I'd like one more belt," Longarm said, "if you don't mind."

"A damn good idea," said the sheriff, pouring another shot into Longarm's glass. "I think I'll join you."

It was dusk. A cool breeze was tugging on Jill's auburn curls as she sat in her small rocker on the veranda balcony. At first she was not sure, but as the rider got closer, she saw it was Kelsey riding in. She had been winding a fresh ball of yarn. Placing it carefully down on the whitewashed railing, she got to her feet and watched as Kelsey rode into the yard and pulled up in front of the barn. She was about to call down a greeting, but Kelsey had seen her on the balcony as he rode in. He smiled coolly up at her and waved briefly as he dismounted and led his horse into the barn.

Jill frowned. She had caught something in Kelsey's manner, a subtle difference in the way he rode in and now the way he strode into the barn, that was unmistakable and just a little troubling. An hour earlier, the blacksmith had returned from Harmony where he had gone for supplies. While there, he had heard of the murder of the Center City telegrapher. So brutal had the killing been, in fact, that many in Harmony were certain the crime had been committed by Bull Schofield.

But Jill knew better. It had been Kelsey, not Bull, whom Harmon had sent to cut those telegraph wires. Jill had been where she was now, on the balcony over the veranda, and had heard Harmon insisting that Kelsey see to cutting those wires. He needed time, he had told Kelsey.

So now he had the time—and a murderer for a son.

Kelsey left the barn and started across the compound toward the ranch house. At that moment Bull left the bunkhouse and called out to him. Kelsey stopped and waited for Bull to join him. The two men stood together conversing quietly. Jill saw Kelsey react in surprise and shock to what Bull had to tell him.

Abruptly, Bull slapped Kelsey encouragingly on the back and the two parted. Kelsey continued on toward the ranch house. Jill knew perfectly well what Bull had just told him. At first Kelsey had seemed crushed, which meant, possibly, that Kelsey had not intended to kill the telegrapher. But as Kelsey neared the ranch house, Jill could see his shoulders squaring almost imperceptibly. When he disappeared at last beneath her into the house, he was walking as straight as a fence post.

This could make for complications, she realized. So far, she had been able to play upon Kelsey's resentment at having to take a back seat to Bull in the running of Jinglebob. Before Kelsey had left on this last errand for his father, in fact, Jill had almost reached an understanding with Kelsey. What she needed to know now was if this new picture Kelsey had of himself altered in any way the relationship she and Kelsey had been fashioning.

The fact that she had allowed herself to be taken in by that fellow she had met on the stage, Custis Long, still rankled with her. When word reached her that he was a U. S. marshal brought in by Bingham, she had almost had a stroke. But the crazy son of a bitch had killed both Clem and Jake, leaving her with no option but to find someone else. She wondered if the big damn fool was still acting unofficially as a range detective for her. Fortunately, she had already acted quickly enough to avert disaster. At any rate, it was this iron necessity to find someone to use against Harmon that had caused her to turn finally to Kelsey, since no matter how desperate she was, there was no way she was going to let Bull Schofield get a hand on her.

And that decision, as it turned out, had met with almost immediate success. That she had not tried to win Kelsey over sooner she now saw as a real blunder. The young man had been putty in her hands all this time, and she had simply not noticed.

Well, now was the time to find out if she still had that hold over him. She left the balcony and went to her room. In front of her dresser mirror, she combed out her hair, putting on each earlobe a touch of that new perfume she had purchased on her last trip to Billings. She gave herself a careful appraisal, decided she was ready for Kelsey, and went down to greet him. Harmon had not yet returned from the Wilkinson place, which gave her an opportunity she had every intention of exploiting.

Kelsey glanced up from the dining-room table as she entered the room. The housekeeper had already placed a hot cup of coffee down before him and was presumably heating something up on the stove. Jill sat down across from him and smiled. "I saw you ride in," she said.

"I saw you up there," he acknowledged.

127

"I missed you."

Kelsey swallowed, then looked straight at her. "Well, I guess I missed you some, too."

"Was your trip a success?"

The housekeeper entered with a platter of steak and eggs and home fries, then returned a moment later with a plate of thick, homemade bread smeared with Kelsey's favorite jelly.

Slicing through his steak, Kelsey looked up at her. "I cut the telegraph lines, like Pa wanted," he told her.

"That's nice."

"Now Pa has all the time he'll need to wrap this valley up. He ain't back yet, huh?"

"No, he isn't."

"Bull told me Jinglebob cattle are already on the Hammer range, and he has a signed bill of sale for Pete Barry's place."

"Looks like things are moving along just fine."

He swallowed. "Yup," he said, as if he had just thought of something he would rather not have. "They surely are."

"Did Bull tell you about the telegrapher in Center City?"

Kelsey stopped chewing and looked directly at Jill. "I don't want to talk about that," he told her.

She felt the chill in his words. "Of course, Kelsey," she told him.

He went back to his food. Like all the Dunstroms, he ate like a famished wolf, with no semblance of table manners. She watched Kelsey a moment longer, the chill in his voice having told her all she needed to know. Then she pushed her chair away from the table and stood up.

He glanced quickly up at her. "Where you goin'?" he asked, a piece of half-chewed steak visible between his teeth as he spoke.

"Upstairs," she told him. "To my room."

Her voice told him unmistakably that she resented his tone, and at once she saw its effect on him. He hastily finished chewing the piece of steak so he could speak. "You think maybe...I could visit you after I finish here?"

"If you want," she told him, her voice no warmer than it had been a moment before.

She had him, she realized exultantly. Now the thing was to reel him in.

He smiled at her. "Okay," he said. "I won't be long. Maybe then we can...talk some."

She leaned close and brushed his still sweaty forehead with her lips. She wanted him to get a whiff of that expensive perfume. "Yes," she said softly, "maybe then we can talk. I'll be waiting."

She turned and moved swiftly from the room. Things were moving fast, she realized, almost too fast. It was becoming difficult for her to hang on. But hang on she would. She had a ranch to win if she did—and much, much more besides.

Kelsey was lying spread-eagled on Jill's bed. The young man was spent. And so, surprisingly, was she. Jill stirred gently, then sat up and slipped into her long gown. Leaving the bed, she walked over to the mirror and picked up her hairbrush. As she brushed, she looked at Kelsey in the mirror.

He was still lying flat on his back, unashamed of his nakedness, his dark pubic patch exposed, his penis, even after all that, still nearly erect. The smell of him remained strong in the room. Had Kelsey been cleaner, it could have been infinitely more enjoyable for her, but she was not going to let that detail detract from the triumph she felt.

During their intimacy, he had told her everything. She had now become his confidante, his soul mate, and she had encouraged him to think this. To her he would come in the future whenever he was troubled or unsure of himself. She had been right in surmising that Kelsey had not realized he had killed the old telegrapher until Bull had told him. At first the knowledge that because of him a man was dead had shaken Kelsey, as she had seen. But it had made him proud, too. He now felt that he could challenge Bull Schofield for priority in running Jinglebob, and he was certain as well that his father would have no choice now but to recognize his worth and reward him accordingly.

"Come over here," Kelsey said to her.

She turned to him. "Say please."

"Please."

She smiled, put her brush down, and returned to the bed. He took her in his arms and kissed her. He still kissed like a little boy, and she was content to leave it like that for now. His hand went to her crotch. She hugged him closer and moved against him.

"You can't," she said. "Not after all that."

"Sure I can," he said with boyish confidence.

But he couldn't, and she had to be kind to him and tell him it was all right. She covered his shoulders and neck and face with kisses. She did this with as much simulated passion as she could manage, but all the time she was recalling that son of a bitch, Custis Long. With him there had been no need to pretend, damn his black heart.

The sound of two horses entering the compound below caused Kelsey to stir suddenly and sit up. "That's Pa ridin' in!" he said, pushing himself off the bed.

She reached over and caught his arm. "Remember," she told him, "let's keep this our secret for now."

He was pulling on his britches. Turning to her, he said, "Sure, Jill. You're right. Pa can be pretty hard to talk to at times." Then he grinned. "It'll be our secret."

"Yes," she said quickly. "That's how I'd like it. At least for now."

He finished pulling on his britches and then went poking around for his boots. As he pulled the first one on, Jill heard Harmon storming up the stairs to his room. As it slammed shut behind him, she looked carefully at Kelsey and saw the first uncertainty he had shown that evening cross his face. He pulled on his other boot a little more slowly and then stood up to slip into his shirt.

"He sure was in a hurry to go to his room," Kelsey commented. "I wonder what's up. Maybe I'll just go downstairs and wait for him in the kitchen."

"Good idea," Jill said.

She watched him slip carefully out of her door and heard not a sound as he moved quickly down the stairs. Going to her door, she opened it a crack and looked out. The door to Harmon's room was still shut. She closed her door and sat back down on her bed. Only then did she allow herself to smile.

* * *

131

Coffee was waiting for Dunstrom on the dining-room table when he had put some pants on and returned downstairs. And Kelsey. He looked up at his father somewhat nervously. Harmon did his best to swallow his frustration. There was no sense in him always beating on his son. The fellow was doing the best he could, he had no doubt.

He nodded curtly to Kelsey and sat down. The coffee was still too hot for him to drink and he looked impatiently toward the kitchen. He was famished. But he could hear the housekeeper rattling pans and knew that food was on the way.

"Pa," Kelsey began, "I done it."

Dunstrom glanced quickly up at his son, and this time he caught something in his narrow face and the watery gray eyes. Was it pride? Gumption? Dunstrom sure as hell hoped so; he had waited a long time to see that. He smiled at his son. "You mean you cut them wires like I told you?" he asked.

"That's right, Pa."

"At how many places?"

Kelsey beamed. "Three. One place they'll find right away, but the other two places will take some doing."

Interested, Dunstrom leaned closer. "What do you mean?"

Kelsey told him how he had cut the wires, then pulled them close together with fishing tackle. As he told his father how he had done it, his enthusiasm grew, and Dunstrom's as well. He was pleasantly surprised at his son's unquestioned initiative. He himself would never have thought of disabling the telegraph so sneakily.

"Where'd you learn that trick, Kelsey?" Dunstrom asked, pleased.

"I read about it. The Confederates did it behind the lines to the Union. Then they sent confusing messages. Really raised hell."

"By Jesus, son, you did great. You gave me the time I need, all right. Now you stay right here. I told Bull to get in here. The three of us are going to use that time, starting first thing tomorrow morning."

"There's one more thing, Pa," Kelsey said, clearing his throat nervously.

Dunstrom caught the sudden change in Kelsey's tone. He looked sharply at him. "Oh? What's that?"

Taking a deep breath, Kelsey told his father about stealing into the telegraph office and knocking out the old telegrapher. Then he told him what he had found out from Bull when he rode in this evening. Dunstrom tried not to show the dismay he felt. On the one hand, he was pleased that Kelsey had been able to act with this kind of decisiveness; on the other, he did not want his boy to hang.

"Just one thing, Kelsey," he said. "Did anyone see you?"

"No one, Pa. Not a soul. I hit Center City just before dawn, and kept out of sight the rest of the time. I returned across country, took the long way around, and came into the valley through the western pass."

"Then there are no witnesses."

"That's right, Pa."

Only then did Dunstrom relax. "Well, then, no harm done. It's too bad about that old fart, but you didn't mean to kill him, right?"

"That's right, Pa," Kelsey said eagerly. "I surely didn't."

"Well, then," Dunstrom said, patting Kelsey approvingly on the arm, "sit back and relax. This'll all be over in a couple of days at the most."

Bull strode into the room, coming from the direction of the kitchen. Behind him came the housekeeper. As soon as she had finished placing Dunstrom's hot meal down before him, Bull joined them at the table and the three settled on the next day's action.

Dunstrom was mightily pleased with the news that Pete Barry's ranch and land was now his. With a snort of satisfaction, he tucked away the bill of sale Bull handed him, after which it was decided that Bull should ride out first thing in the morning to see to that fool Wilkinson and his daughter.

After he returned, the foreman would join Dunstrom and Kelsey when they rode out to settle matters finally with Nate Simpson and Ben Overmeyer. Both ranchers had made sounds indicating they just might sell out, after all. If so, there would be no trouble. Otherwise, Dunstrom would be sided by Kelsey and most of the Jinglebob riders, including Bull. Just as with Pete Barry, Dunstrom had no doubt the two cattlemen would see the wisdom of selling out and moving on.

With the next day's plans settled, Bull and Kelsey got up from their chairs and left Dunstrom alone to finish eating. As Dunstrom pitched into his overdue supper, there was a grim smile on his face. Tomorrow promised to be a very profitable day.

Chapter 8

Pete Barry was waiting for Longarm in the lobby of the Territorial House when the deputy marshal came down the next morning. It wasn't really morning yet. The sun was just a tentative glow in the eastern sky.

"What is it, Pete?" Longarm asked.

"I got a message from that kid the sheriff sent out yesterday."

"Let's have it."

Pete handed it to Longarm. The message was written in pencil on the back of a piece of wrapping paper and was barely legible. It read:

Sheriff Bingham:
    Just leave us be, Sheriff. We have our own plans for taking care of that son of a bitch, Dunstrom.

There were two signatures at the bottom of the message, those of Ben Overmeyer and Nate Simpson.

"Thanks, Pete," Longarm said, pocketing the message. "I'll give it to the sheriff when I see him."

"We still going out after Bull?" Pete asked.

"As far as I know. You eaten yet?"

"Yeah, I've eaten."

"Well, I haven't, and I'm supposed to meet the sheriff across the street in the restaurant. Come on," Longarm said.

Pete fell in beside Longarm as the tall lawman strode from the hotel and started across the street. "There's something maybe you and the sheriff ought to know, Marshal," Pete said.

"What's that?"

"That kid who brought the message back from Overmeyer and Simpson rode in late last night, then rode right back out again with a wagon load of goods he purchased from the general store."

"That so?"

Pete nodded. "Yup. I spoke to Willett, the owner of the store. He was fit to be tied. Said that kid got him up in the middle of the night to help him load the wagon. And you know what it was he loaded onto the wagon, Marshal?"

Entering the restaurant, Longarm caught sight of the sheriff already ordering his breakfast. Longarm sat down across from Bingham. "Start me off with coffee," he told the waitress.

Pete pulled up beside the table and looked down at Longarm. "Don't you want to know what was in that wagon, Marshal?"

"Of course, Pete. What was it?"

"Blasting powder."

Longarm looked up at the waitress. "Forget the coffee. Just bring me whatever the sheriff is having—and hurry it up."

As the waitress hurried into the kitchen, Longarm told Pete to sit down. He wanted more details. Pete provided them. "The wagon was rented from the livery stable, and the owners of the Lazy S and the Circle O paid for it."

At this juncture, Longarm handed the sheriff the note the kid had brought back from the two cattlemen. The sheriff read it quickly, then crumpled it.

"No doubt about what they got in mind," he said.

Longarm nodded. "They're going to blow Dunstrom's dam. Things are heating up pretty fast, I'd say."

Pete cleared his throat. "There's just one more thing."

Both men turned to Pete.

"Willett knew right away where that blasting powder was going and why. Jinglebob's his best customer in this valley. And if things go on the way they been goin', pretty soon Jinglebob might end up his only customer."

"Go on, Pete," said Longarm.

"Willett knows which side his bread is buttered on. So last night he sent the town marshal out to the Jinglebob to warn Dunstrom."

"Oh, Jesus," muttered Bingham.

Longarm cocked an eyebrow at Pete. "You got anything more you want to tell us, Pete?"

"Nope," the young man said grimly. "That's it."

"Well, that's enough," said the sheriff. "The fat's in the fire, sure enough. As soon as Slim tells Harmon

Dunstrom what them two ranchers're up to, he'll go after them in force."

"I say we ride for that dam first thing," said Longarm. "See if we can't stop them two cattlemen before it's too late."

"Or at least join them if it is," said Pete grimly. "Maybe we can clean Bull's clock while we're at it."

"Do you know where the dam is?" Longarm asked Pete.

"Sure."

"All right, Pete," said the sheriff. "Sit down and have a cup of coffee with us. Another two minutes won't hurt. Then we're going to have to ride. Maybe we can get up there in time to stop the James county war before it begins."

Kelsey kissed Jill as hard as he could, then chuckled and pushed himself off her. He felt deliciously spent, as light as a feather. But Jill just lay on her back, and she hadn't really responded to the kiss.

He propped his cheek up on his palm and gazed at her, his eyes glowing maliciously. "What's the matter?" he asked roughly.

"Nothing."

"Wasn't I big enough this time?"

Jill turned her back on him and pulled the sheet up over her nakedness. Kelsey reached over quickly, grabbed her shoulder, and snapped her back around to face him.

"Come on!" he said. "You got any complaints? Out with it! Pa says you been to bed with just about everybody in this here county. You've been plowed by experts. I want to know how I compare."

"Damn you! Damn you *and* your father!"

Kelsey slapped her hard. She did not raise her hand to feel her stinging face.

"Well, well, well," she said through clenched lips. "Now I know what it looks like to see a worm turn. A *real* worm. All right, little boy. Let me tell you how you compare. You don't compare at all! When you're inside me all I can think of is that federal marshal I had the night before you and Bull came to take me back here. Now there was a man who knew how to take care of a woman!"

Kelsey didn't want to hear any more. He clapped a hand over Jill's mouth. She bit his palm. With a suppressed howl, he pulled his hand back, then scrambled off the bed. He stood there holding his bleeding hand, naked and shivering in the chill of her room, while she grinned at him, her eyes blazing in fury.

"Let me tell you something, Kelsey," she went on, warming to her topic. "You ain't big enough down there. And I don't think you ever will be. You got to be a *man* to fill a woman, and that ain't never going to happen!"

"You shut up now! I'm warnin' you!"

She pulled back in feigned surprise. "But I thought you wanted to know how you compare! Don't you want to know that, Kelsey?"

"It ain't true, what you just said. It's your fault! You're too big. Like my Pa warned me! He said plowing you is like plowing a rain barrel!"

With a snarl she jumped off the bed and drew her hooked fingers down the length of his face. Screaming, he grabbed at her hands. She yanked free of him contemptuously.

"Get out of my room, Kelsey," she told him, her voice low and terrible. "And don't you ever come in here again. If you do, I'll cut you. I'll slice you right down the middle with a fish knife I keep handy—the same one I keep in case your father comes in here. Now, get!"

He snatched up his dressing gown and fled her room. She went to the door after him and locked it. Then she went to her closet and took out her rifle. It was, as always, well oiled and in excellent condition. Raised on a ranch in Colorado, she not only knew how to ride, but how to shoot. And how to kill.

Still seething, Jill went to the window. The yard was quiet, a stark contrast to her own furious unrest. Earlier, Bull had ridden out with a large contingent of riders to subdue the Wilkinson ranch. When Kelsey had told her what they were about, she'd had difficulty suppressing her laughter—especially when Kelsey revealed why Harmon had come in so late the day before, then rushed up to his room immediately.

She had been such a fool to trust Kelsey. She had miscalculated badly. Secure now in his father's esteem, the young whelp had gone straight to Harmon to crow about his conquest, even though Kelsey had promised her that he would not tell anyone. And of course Harmon did not waste any time at all in blackening her in Kelsey's eyes. So Kelsey had come in here this morning as a man would come to a whore, and had treated her accordingly.

She still shuddered at the memory of it. What was there about men that saw nothing wrong if they slept with anyone they could, but thought a woman a whore if she was good enough to accept them? It did not matter now. She had been a fool to think she could take what was hers by working through that whelp. She would have to take it her own way.

The same way Harmon was planning to take this valley from the other ranchers.

She was turning away from the window when she heard the hoofbeats of a rider coming hard. Looking back out the window, she saw Harmony's town marshal riding in. As he pulled up in the yard, the wrangler left the barn and hurried over to him. Another ranch hand came running also.

Jill frowned. For Slim to have arrived here this early in the day meant he must have ridden through the night, or at least have spent the night on the trail. As she watched, Slim dismounted swiftly and hurried toward the ranch house. Jill put her rifle back in her closet, slipped into her nightgown, and hurried from her room.

A moment later, standing on the balcony over the veranda, she heard Slim telling Harmon that Simpson and Overmeyer were planning to blow up the dam Harmon had built. She heard Harmon's incredulous oath as he asked Slim for the details, then heard him yell for Kelsey and instruct one of the hands to ride after Bull and give him the news. Then he told the wrangler to tell those hands who had not left earlier with Bull to saddle up.

She stood for a moment, smiling in grim satisfaction, then turned and hurried back to her room.

By mid-morning Longarm, the sheriff, and Pete Barry were well on their way to Dunstrom's dam. It was located northwest of Harmony, and the quickest, most direct route to it was through Red Notch. Since the dam was closer to Harmony than it was to the Jinglebob ranch, Longarm was confident they would have no difficulty reaching it before Dunstrom did—assuming, as the three of them had to, that the owner of the Jinglebob would waste no time now moving on the Lazy S and on Ben Overmeyer.

Since they were passing close by the Wilkinson place by this time, Longarm suggested they stop at the ranch to make sure Kitty and her father were all right. He had begun to worry about Kitty and her father the moment he heard what had happened to Pete Barry. And there might be some fresh coffee in it for them, as well.

As they turned off the trail and headed toward the Wilkinson ranch, Pete spurred ahead of them. Longarm pulled his horse closer to Sheriff Bingham's.

"Tex, what would you say if I told you Jill Dunstrom is certain Harmon Dunstrom killed his brother Dennis, her husband, in order to gain full control of Jinglebob?"

"She tell you that, did she?" the sheriff asked.

"She also said she was certain the Warrens were a party to Dennis's murder."

"Interesting. And why did she tell you all this, Longarm?"

"She wanted me to act as a sort of range detective for her, to find out how Harmon is cheating her out of her rightful inheritance. At the time, of course, she had no idea I was a deputy U. S. marshal."

"You turned her down, did you?"

"Not entirely. I said I would keep my eyes open. What I would like is your opinion. This Harmon Dunstrom is an arrogant enough son of a bitch. But do you think he could have had his own brother killed?"

142

"Sure. Without blinking an eye."

"Then Jill was telling the truth," Longarm said thoughtfully.

"I didn't say that. I didn't say that at all." Bingham looked at Longarm, a light suddenly dancing in his eyes. "Did you take her to bed that night you two rolled in?"

"I don't have to answer that, do I?"

"Nope. But you don't need to, either. What I'm sayin', Longarm, is that Jill Dunstrom is not to be trusted. If I said she was as crooked as a sidewinder and as horny as a toad, I'd be telling you only the half of it. She is also a very dangerous woman."

"Would you like to enlarge on that, Sheriff?"

"Sure. If anyone paid the Warrens to kill Dennis Dunstrom, it wasn't Harmon, as cold-blooded as he is. It was Jill Dunstrom."

"She said Harmon did it because he wanted her so badly," Longarm said.

"Nope. Harmon Dunstrom would cheerfully wring her neck, but he hasn't yet thought of a way he could do it without getting hung for his trouble. I've watched that man when her name is mentioned or when she's in sight of him. Harmon Dunstrom has a gut-deep loathing for Jill Dunstrom, and that's not something a man can hide."

"What you are saying is that Jill Dunstrom is not what she appears."

"Nor is she as pure as the driven snow," said the sheriff with a snort.

"I have allowed a pretty woman to turn my head," Longarm said.

"And foul up your judgment," the sheriff agreed. "She is not the kind of woman whose honor I would dispute

143

with the likes of Bull Schofield. What we all figured was you did the right thing for the wrong reasons."

"I guess that's some comfort," Longarm said.

"Another thing: there were only three stage holdups in the past year, and Jill was on the stage each time. Curious, wouldn't you say?"

Longarm frowned. "I see what you mean. An odd but effective way to pay someone off. Just let them hold you up every once in a while."

"Yes. I was thinking the same damn thing. But why in blazes would Jill be paying off the Warrens?"

Something occurred to Longarm almost immediately, but before he could say anything, Pete, still riding well ahead of them, looked back and pointed. "Over there!" he called. "A fire!"

Longarm looked where Pete was pointing and saw, just over the next rise, a dark plume of smoke pumping into the sky. Lifting their mounts to a gallop, they topped the rise and saw that it was Wilkinson's ranch house and barn that were burning. The fire was eating rapidly through both buildings by this time, the thick black smoke's underbelly a livid, hellish red.

Standing back from the burning buildings watching calmly were Jinglebob riders. Bull had shown surprising restraint, however. The Wilkinsons' spring wagon had been pulled to safety before the barn had been set ablaze, and their two horses had been let out into the pasture below the ranch. Off to one side, under the guns of a Jinglebob gunslick, huddled Kitty and her father. Wilkinson was not on his feet. He was sitting crookedly on a low rock, Kitty by his side, her hand resting on his shoulder.

There was a muffled roar as the roof went up. Long-arm saw Kitty turn away from the flames and bury her face in her hands.

"I guess that hunch of yours was on target, Longarm," said the sheriff glumly.

"He's down there," said Pete. "I can see the son of a bitch."

"Bull Schofield?" the sheriff asked.

"That's right," said Pete, his mouth a thin, bitter line.

"Easy now," Longarm told him. "Keep your britches on. I count eight men down there, not including Bull. We better think our next move over real careful. I say we take cover, then move closer. So far we got surprise on our side. Let's move."

Dismounting swiftly, they hobbled their horses in a small clearing, then moved down the slope toward the burning ranch, keeping low and using the rocks for cover. By the time they were within a hundred yards of the Wilkinson place, the flames had died some, but there was still a thick, roiling column of smoke pumping skyward.

Two of the Jinglebob riders had swung back into their saddles to get a better view. The others were standing about in small groups, sniggering and joking as they watched. So far, this morning's chore had amounted to little more than a pleasant diversion for them—though from time to time Longarm caught one or two of them glancing nervously over at Kitty and her father.

Bull Schofield stood apart, his feet braced widely, his arms folded, while he watched. From the tilt of his head and the set to his shoulders, it was obvious he was quite pleased with himself.

Pulling up within easy range of the nearest Jinglebob riders, Longarm took all this in and felt the same unmanageable rage that he knew must now be burning within Kitty and her father. He glanced to his right. Pete was crouching down behind a low tangle of juniper. On his left the sheriff was getting comfortable behind a low, flat boulder.

"Cover me," said Longarm.

He levered a fresh cartridge into his rifle's firing chamber, stepped out from the pines, and started to walk over the uneven ground. Every Jinglebob rider was watching the burning buildings and the sound of the flames covered the crunch of Longarm's footsteps on the rocky ground. He kept walking. Soon he was able to see clearly the stitching on a few of the men's boots. And still he kept walking.

Kitty turned to look at Bull and picked out Longarm's advancing figure at the same time. He saw her catch herself, then turn quickly back around and say something to her father. The old man appeared to shrink noticeably, then brace himself. Longarm could guess what Kitty had told him. In a few seconds there would be lead flying and he should get ready to dive for cover.

But Longarm did not intend to start shooting. Not if he could make a few more yards without being discovered. Then he would be close enough to take Bull without firing a shot. It was a chance worth taking.

The horse forked by one of the Jinglebob riders shied nervously. It must have sensed Longarm's approach. The rider glanced quickly in Longarm's direction. Letting out a warning cry to the others, he clawed for his gun. A rifle cracked from the rocks behind Longarm and the rider toppled from his mount.

Longarm went down on one knee and brought his rifle up as the rest of the hands flung themselves about and started firing at him. Longarm returned the fire of the other rider, knocking him out of his saddle. By that time Longarm could have walked on the lead pouring over his head. Flinging himself flat, he levered swiftly and returned the fire. His fire combined with that of Bingham and Pete Barry scattered the Jinglebob riders. It was clear they had no idea how many guns backed Longarm and were intent only on getting away. In the confusion, Longarm realized that Bull Schofield had vanished. Almost as quickly, the Jinglebob riders had galloped from the ranch, firing wildly in Longarm's general direction as they went.

It was over as swiftly as it had begun. Longarm got to his feet and saw Kitty and her father huddled on the ground. At the sight of Longarm's standing figure, Kitty hauled her father upright.

Longarm walked over to her. "Sorry, Kitty. It looks like we got here too late."

At that moment Kitty's father turned to look at him. Longarm felt suddenly sick. The old man had been battered cruelly about the head and shoulders. From the look of it, his nose was broken, and he seemed to be having difficulty breathing.

"My God, Kitty. What happened to your father?" Longarm asked.

"Bull Schofield happened to him," she said bitterly, tears gleaming in her eyes. As she spoke, she reached out to steady her father.

The old man grinned feebly at Longarm. "I'll live," he managed. "That's the trouble."

"You need help," Longarm said.

"I think his ribs are broken," Kitty said.

Even as she spoke, her father began to cough, doubling over painfully each time. Kitty gently eased him back down onto the boulder they had been huddling behind a moment before.

Longarm heard the sheriff shout to him. He turned. Bingham was running hard toward him, alone.

"Where's Pete?" Longarm asked, as Bingham pulled up beside them.

"He's gone after Bull. There was no way I could stop him."

Longarm's first reaction was anger, then he shrugged. "Hell, why try to stop him? Do you know the way to that dam from here?"

"I can find it."

"All right, then. Now, take a look at Wilkinson. More of Bull Schofield's handiwork. Before we light out for that dam, I think we better take Kitty and her father to Minnie Compson's. Her ranch isn't far from here."

"All right. But what about those two Jinglebob riders over there?"

Longarm glanced over and saw one man sitting up dazedly. A little farther on, another was sprawled face-down.

"How bad are they?" he asked.

"One's dead, the other's got a smashed shoulder," the sheriff replied.

"Can the one with the bad shoulder ride?" Longarm asked.

"Maybe."

"Let him take his dead pal back to Jinglebob, then. Harmon can bury him."

As Bingham walked over to the wounded Jinglebob rider, Longarm and Kitty helped Wilkinson over to the spring wagon.

The drive to the Bar C was painstakingly slow. The spring wagon was in miserable shape, and each unyielding bump caused Kitty's father to groan or cry out. As a result, it took them almost two hours to reach the Compson ranch, but when they did, Minnie Compson proved to be as generous and as eager to help as Longarm had assured Kitty she would be. In less than an hour Minnie had bound Wilkinson's ribs, put him to bed, given Kitty a fresh dress to put on, and assured Longarm and Bingham that they could leave Kitty and her father at the Bar C in perfect confidence.

When Longarm reminded her that Harmon Dunstrom had now thrown off all restraint in his drive to take over the valley, the woman simply pointed to her loaded shotgun leaning against the wall.

Riding out, heading northwest for the dam once more, Bingham nudged his horse closer to Longarm's.

"Longarm," he said, "I like that Minnie Compson. She's a woman a man could respect and love—and both at the same time."

"I'll tell her you said that."

"No. When the time comes, I'll tell her."

Longarm glanced at the sheriff. There was a question

he had to ask the man, one that by this time he did not really want to ask. But they had just gone into battle, so to speak, and it was more than likely there would be another one before this day was out, and the chance might not come again.

"Tex," he began gently, "have you ever heard of a jasper named Bart Bonham?"

Watching Bingham closely, Longarm thought he saw the man flinch.

"Yup," Bingham said.

"Then you know another reason why I'm here—besides helping you stop this here battle with Jinglebob and the other ranchers."

"I do now."

"My chief's name in Denver is Billy Vail. He's the one sent me to bring you in."

Bingham looked at Longarm in open astonishment. "Did you say Billy Vail? He's the U. S. marshal in Denver City?"

Longarm nodded. "You know Billy, do you?" Longarm asked.

"Hell, yes, I remember Billy Vail. He was Charlie's favorite uncle. He sprung us from Yuma. If he's the U.S. marshal in Denver, he sure as hell has come a long way since then."

"You admit killing Charlie Vail?"

"I killed him, all right. I had no choice."

"Billy says you killed Charlie for his horse. They found him dead and his horse gone. Yours had gone lame. You don't dispute that?"

"What good would it do if I did?" Abruptly Bingham shrugged. "But maybe I owe you an explanation, at least."

"I'd like to hear it."

"Charlie and I hadn't gone more'n a couple of miles before he complained about the mount Billy gave him. So we swapped horses. But it didn't do any good. Charlie drove the horse too hard and it pulled up lame. When I caught up to him he was sitting on a rock starin' at the horse he had just shot."

They were approaching an arroyo, and Bingham turned his complete attention to guiding his horse through it. For a while the two men rode in single file. Once they were through, Bingham caught up to Longarm.

"Go on," said Longarm.

"Well, with Charlie's horse dead, that left only one horse between us. I offered to ride double, but Charlie wouldn't hear of it. He didn't want to share a horse. He was crazy to get away. And after all, it was his uncle who had sprung us and got us the horses, so he figured he had a right to my horse. I tried to reason with him, but it didn't do any good. We both drew at the same time. I was luckier than he was, that's all."

Frowning, Longarm considered Bingham's account of what happened. He found nothing in it to conflict with what Billy Vail had already told him.

"It makes sense, I suppose," Longarm said.

"It would make even more sense if you knew Charlie Vail. As it stands now, it's just my word against a dead man's. I don't figure Billy Vail would have any reason for believing me. Where Charlie was concerned, he didn't see very clear."

"I'll still have to bring you in."

"You know what, Longarm? It'll be a relief to me. That dead man I left back on the desert has been haunting me all these years—the way it has been haunting Billy, I suppose. But I sure never figured Billy Vail would turn out to be a lawman." Bingham peered closely at Longarm. "Just how in hell did he find me, anyway?"

"That letter you sent to Washington. He compared your signature with the one on a bill of sale you signed."

"Bill of sale?" the sheriff asked.

"Sure. For the horse—the one you let Charlie ride."

"You mean he kept that bill of sale all this time?"

"He did."

Bingham shook his head in wonder. Then he chuckled silently and smiled in obvious appreciation of Billy Vail's uncanny patience.

Longarm decided to say no more. He had hoped against hope that the sheriff was not the man Billy Vail had been hoping to track all these years. The fact that Billy was right, that Sheriff Tex Bingham was in reality Bart Bonham, did not please Longarm at all. Watching the sheriff as he rode beside him, Longarm was struck by the strength he saw reflected in the older man's countenance. He was now, certainly, as good and as honest a lawman as Billy Vail himself.

What in hell was it, Longarm wondered in honest bafflement, that turned men onto the paths they chose?

"Here we are," Bingham said a moment later, pulling up.

Longarm reined in his horse also. They had entered a high-walled canyon, and just ahead of them was a strangely quiet, completely dry river bed. Not a single trickle ran down through its center. At this altitude, with all the many snow-clad peaks enclosing the valley, the walls of this canyon should have been echoing to a young river's lusty, brawling roar.

Longarm shook his head in amazement. "It must have taken some doing to dam up this stream," he said.

Bingham nodded. "Harmon didn't spare any expense. He used some of the engineers he brought in to build that slaughterhouse. Maybe that's why he ran out of money—using it for crazy, mean projects like this."

"Let's go upstream and get as close to the dam as we can to see what's going on. So far, it's been pretty quiet."

Bingham nodded. "So far. But I wouldn't count on it staying that way."

Longarm knew what Bingham meant. At any moment there might be a shuddering explosion above them, followed by a wall of water thundering down through this canyon, sweeping everything before it.

Including any riders foolish enough to get caught in its path.

Chapter 9

Pete Barry settled himself in behind the boulder and levered a fresh cartridge into his Winchester's firing chamber. Perched high on a ridge, he watched the approach of Bull Schofield and the rest of the riders who had managed to escape that firefight at Wilkinson's ranch. They were on their way through a narrow defile at least a couple of hundred yards down the trail. Once they broke out of these badlands they would be close to the river, the other side of which marked the legal boundaries of Jinglebob range. Not that Harmon Dunstrom had ever paid any attention to such niceties.

Pete made himself comfortable and waited for Bull to get closer. It had taken him some hard riding to circle around ahead of Bull like this, and he did not want to waste that effort by firing too soon.

A rider appeared on the trail below, sweeping up from the river, heading into the badlands. Pulling up suddenly atop a small ridge, he peered down the trail. Almost at once he spotted Bull and the rest of the Jinglebob riders. Spurring his horse to a gallop, he headed for them.

Cursing bitterly, Pete watched as Bull rode forward to meet the oncoming rider. There was no doubt in his mind that this was a Jinglebob rider, and he could almost hear what he was telling Bull. It had to do with that load of black powder shipped to Nate Simpson and Ben Overmeyer. As Pete watched in dismay, he saw Bull halt the riders, then motion for them to swing back through the hills. In a moment they had all lifted their mounts to a gallop and disappeared behind a plume of dust. When it settled the trail was empty.

Pete got to his feet, cursing bitterly, and angled swiftly down the steep slope to the clearing where he had hobbled his mount.

Jill waited until the ranch was empty except for the housekeeper before she saddled her favorite black and rode out.

Even the cook and the wrangler were gone. Harmon had demanded that every hand left on the ranch ride out with him and Kelsey. But this still gave him only four riders besides himself and Kelsey. Jill understood his urgency. The only real hold Harmon had over those two ranchers was that dam. With it blown to hell and gone, they could stall for at least another year. And that would ruin Harmon's big plans.

Jill knew where the dam was. She had ridden out

many times to watch it being built. The engineer working for Harmon had claimed a dam at that spot was impossible, but Harmon had insisted, and the engineer had finally managed to do it. The stream leading from the huge lake impounded behind the dam now sluiced back down the other side of the mountain and flowed into the larger stream that cut through the valley—the same stream that fed Jinglebob range, which meant Harmon had it both ways. He had managed to shut off the flow to Overmeyer and Simpson, while at the same time he had increased the flow to his own stream.

Jill did not make any attempt to overtake Harmon. She had long since discovered a shorter, more direct route to the dam. Before long, she was beginning to notice familiar landmarks and left the trail she had been following to cut into steeper country, heading for a spot she knew of that would give her a clear, unobstructed view of the dam.

She had been a fool to rely on the Warrens, now that she thought of it. In a way, she should be grateful to that federal marshal for taking them out of the picture. They had started to become nuisances, especially Clem Warren. She knew what to do now, and she could do it. And the thought of Kelsey's brutality toward her that morning, especially his searing insolence, made her more than willing—anxious, even—to take things into her own hands at last.

She patted the rifle in her scabbard, and then leaned forward in her saddle to ease her back as the horse pulled still higher into the rocks.

* * *

157

Nate Simpson pulled the team to a halt, wound the reins about the brake handle, and jumped down. Astride a big chestnut, Ben Overmeyer reined up beside the wagon, dismounted, and walked with Nate to the rear of the wagon.

"You're sure this is as close as we can get?" Ben asked Nate.

"Yes, damn it, I'm sure. That wagon's about ready to fall apart, and if we go any steeper, the powder's liable to break loose."

Ben nodded unhappily and glanced at the slope ahead of them. He supposed Nate was right, but that didn't make it any easier for him to take. They still had a long, miserable trek to reach the underside of Dunstrom's dam. And then they would have to plant the goddamn powder right under the nose of the two guards Dunstrom had posted.

Of the two men, Nate was the taller, a lean, stringy fellow with a lantern jaw and pale blue eyes. He wore washed-out Levi's, a checked shirt and buttonless vest, and a battered gray Stetson. Unlike Ben, he had a sixgun strapped to his waist. He had been running the Lazy S alone save for the unreliable assistance of a beat-up cowpoke who had quit two weeks before when he saw this trouble with Jinglebob brewing. Nate was married, but his wife had up and left him seven years before, taking his three children, all girls, with her. At times Nate did not know whether to go down on his knees and thank God for his deliverance or to cry his heart out that he should be so lonely and bereft. He managed to keep going and do neither.

Ben was Nate's opposite, a short, stocky man with dark, bushy hair. He favored a black, floppy-brimmed hat and broad yellow braces. He had never employed a hired hand. A confirmed bachelor, he lived in his sprawling ranch house amidst an amazing clutter of old and broken things, each of which he prized. He was the biggest pack rat Nate had ever seen.

The two got along famously. Their ranches adjoined, and they had no difficulty working together. Each could count entirely on the other whenever a need arose. In a curious way their ranches functioned almost as a single entity, so closely did the two cattlemen cooperate.

This did not mean, however, that they never argued. Indeed, they debated almost every move fiercely. But whenever they reached a decision they stuck to it. This decision to blow the dam had been hammered out over a two-week period, and though Ben was unhappy at the brute labor involved—not to mention the danger—there was no holding back. They were both equally determined to destroy Dunstrom and his illegal dam.

"I still wish to hell he could wait until it gets dark," Ben said gloomily, peering up the slope.

"Hell, Ben, so do I. But you heard what that kid said. Willett sent the town marshal out to tell Dunstrom what we're up to. By tonight this slope will be swarming with Jinglebob riders."

Ben nodded gloomily. He and Nate had been all over this in the past hour. Even if they hid the powder and waited to blow the dam, it would not do any good. Once Dunstrom knew what they were up to he would not rest until he had driven them from the valley. If they were going to act at all, they would have to act now—before Dunstrom and his men reached this dam.

Ben sighed and looked nervously about him. "How much time do you think we have, Nate?"

"I told you. We've got enough time. Even if Slim got to the Jinglebob this morning, Dunstrom has a way to go yet. I say we've got another two hours at least."

Ben nodded unhappily. "So let's get on with it."

Nate reached into the wagon for the long coil of Bickford fuses and slung it over his shoulder. Then he hefted a barrel of black powder onto his shoulder and started up the slope.

Ben reached in for another barrel and followed Nate. A great overhanging slab of rock projected out over the trail they were taking, completely blocking off from their view the dam toward which they were toiling. But they had decided on this route, despite its steepness and the treacherous footing caused by the talus, since it offered them protection from above. Just as they could not see the dam, the two guards stationed above them could not see them either.

After a good half hour both men had reached the base of the dam, a crude but efficient framework of logs braced solidly against the sheer canyon walls on either side. Interspersed between the logs and packed in solidly was an efficient mixture of mud and brush and clay that had hardened close to the consistency of cement.

"Better hold up a minute," said Nate softly, as Ben reached him. "I'll peek out and see if I can see either of them."

Ben, puffing hard, simply nodded.

Putting the barrel of black powder down carefully, Nate slipped out from under the overhang and, taking cover behind a juniper bush, peered up at the lip of the dam. On some days, the two guards could be seen standing in full view, gazing down at the silent watercourse far below.

But this time Nate did not see a guard—not one. He waited patiently for a while, to be sure. Then he returned to Ben.

"All clear so far," he said.

Nate hefted the barrel back up onto his shoulder and braced himself. They would have to dart out from their present cover to reach the dam's underpinning. For those few seconds they would be visible from above. Nate went first. There was no cry from the dam above them. Ben followed him just as quickly, and again there was no outcry.

Once they had worked their way in under the lashed timbers, they were confident that they could not be seen from the walkway on the dam above them. Nate placed the first barrel in a convenient opening and wedged it in gently. As Nate fixed the fuse to his barrel, Ben worked his way past him and placed his barrel just as carefully about ten yards farther down. This made for two barrels of black powder placed less than twenty yards apart.

In all, the two men had purchased five barrels of black powder. Nate planned to use them all, which meant they would have to go back for the others. Nate had argued that it was not likely that two charges alone would be sufficient. And the other barrels would have to be placed farther out, with at least two of them set directly under the center of the dam, where the greatest weight of water rested.

Nate finished attaching the fuses, stashed what fuse remained nearby, then led the way back to the trail. He made it successfully, but a rifle high above them spoke sharply just as Ben darted from cover.

Nate spun, his heart in his mouth. A second rifle cracked. Ben faltered, his eyes going suddenly wide in terror. To Nate it looked as if an invisible hand had smashed his knees out from under him. His chest struck the slanting ground first, then the side of his head. For a terrible moment he lay still, then he raised his head feebly.

"Nate!" he called. "Nate! I'm hit!"

Nate raced back over the open ground and, grabbing Ben by his arms, yanked him upright, then folded him over his shoulder. The talus at Nate's feet was whining shrilly by this time from the near constant fusillade pouring down from above. Staggering under Ben's weight, Nate fled back to the protection of the overhang as two more quick shots rang out.

Before he reached it, he heard the thunk of another round striking Ben and felt the warm gout of blood that swept down his back, plastering his shirt to it. Reaching the protection of the overhang, he lowered Ben to the ground. The man's eyes were closed, and he was breathing with difficulty. A thin line of blood began to trace a path from one corner of his mouth.

Nate was close to tears. He was so upset he didn't know which way to turn. Their rifles were in the wagon below. He wanted—he needed—to get his, but he did

162

not want to leave Ben. Yet carrying him down the slope would take so much time. It would give those two bastards above him all the time they needed to move down and finish them off.

Ben opened his eyes. "Get our rifles, Nate!" he wheezed painfully. "Go ahead. Give me your Colt. I'll hold them off while you go."

Nate nodded quickly, handed Ben his Colt, then turned and scrambled swiftly back down the slope. He lost control twice and sprawled headlong, but picked himself up each time without caring and kept going. As he reached the wagon and grabbed his rifle, he heard Ben firing at the approaching guards.

Nate turned and flung himself back up the slope.

Longarm pulled up. "Did you hear that?"

"I did," said Bingham. "Gunfire—up close to the dam."

The two men said nothing more as they spurred their horses on up the trail. Soon, however, the going became so difficult that Longarm cut off the trail and headed up the riverbed, Bingham following after him. Here the pockets of sand and gravel caused some difficulty, but the horses were still able to make better time than if they had stayed on the trail hugging the canyon wall.

The chance that the dam would go while they were racing up the dry riverbed was something Longarm preferred not to think about.

Longarm saw the wagon first. He charged up the steep embankment and dismounted beside it. The firing, sporadic now, was coming from directly above. Glancing into the wagon, the two men spotted three barrels of black powder.

"Looks like Nate and Ben got caught setting the charges," said Bingham.

"Let's see if we can't help them out," Longarm said, scrambling up the slope.

It was a long climb, but at last they were close enough to hear the spent rounds striking the ground or cutting through the branches. Holding up, Longarm peered around a stand of piñon that clung to a gravel slope. He saw two men lying behind an imbedded, cinder-like stone. One was lying flat and had a Colt in his hand. The other one was using a rifle and had pulled himself up so that he could fire over the boulder.

Beside him, Bingham said, "That's Ben Overmeyer with the Colt, and Nate's the one with the rifle."

The two men were so busy returning fire from above that they had not heard Longarm and Bingham approach. Longarm pulled back. He was afraid he would inadvertently draw their fire. In their present situation they would undoubtedly fire first and ask questions later.

"You better call out to them," he told Bingham.

Bingham tried once, without success. Then he called again, a bit louder. Nate spun around and caught sight of the sheriff. Bingham waved. Nate seemed pathetically glad to see him. He turned swiftly and, keeping low, ran down the slope.

"Ben's hit. I think he's hurt bad. I can't leave him," he said to them.

"How many you fighting off?" Longarm asked.

"Two, but I think I winged one of them. Their fire has slackened off since."

"Go back to Ben. The sheriff here will go with you to keep up the fire. I'll climb up there and see if I can surprise Dunstrom's men."

Nate nodded and he and Bingham moved back to Ben.

As the two men began once again to return the fire from above, Longarm pulled himself up through the pines. When he gone so high that he could see through the trees the huge, gleaming lake backed up behind the dam, he turned and moved cautiously back down the slope toward it. Guided by the sound of sporadic rifle fire ahead of him, he kept going until he spotted the two Jinglebob guards. They were on top of the dam, firing steadily down at Nate's position.

Nate was right—he had winged one of them. The wounded Jinglebob guard was sitting up painfully, his left arm holding his right shoulder. The wound looked pretty bloody, as if the round had crunched some bone and then torn up a lot of muscle. The wounded one was paying little attention to his companion. He was leaning back against a pile of timber left over from the construction of the dam, his head back, his eyes closed.

The other guard was stretched out flat on the ground, levering and firing steadily, but with seemingly little enthusiasm. Obviously, he was just trying to keep Nate pinned until help arrived.

Longarm moved swiftly around behind the rifleman, then levered a fresh cartridge into his firing chamber and strode toward them.

"Drop it," he told the man who was shooting.

The Jinglebob guard turned his head, saw Longarm, and dropped the rifle.

"Where the hell did you come from?" he wanted to

know. "I was sure there were only two of you."

Without bothering to answer him, Longarm took the man's rifle and flung it into the canyon. Then he took the Jinglebob hand's sidearm and that of his wounded companion, and tossed them after the rifle. A quick examination of the wounded guard followed.

"This buddy of yours is hurt bad," he said to the first one. "Find your horses and get him to Harmony. There's a doctor there."

The man appeared to hesitate.

"Go on!" Longarm told him. "Unless you want to stay here and die with him."

The fellow shrugged. "I'll get the horses," he said.

A moment later, as the two riders disappeared in the direction of Harmony, Longarm called down the slope to tell them the dam was cleared and to warn them that he was on his way down the slope. When he reached the two men, Bingham told him that Ben Overmeyer was dead.

Longarm knelt quickly by the cattleman and saw that it was true. He shook his head and stood up. There were unashamed tears in Nate's eyes. Longarm took a deep breath. "Well, Nate," he asked, "what do you want to do?"

"I want to finish what Ben and I started," he said.

Longarm looked at Bingham. "I say why not? There'll be no peace in this valley until Dunstrom is stopped. And blowing this dam is a good beginning."

"You'll get no argument from me on that," Bingham said grimly. "Let's get to work."

* * *

Pete Barry had heard the gunfire. It came from behind him, echoing like sporadic thunder in the surrounding hills. Bull heard the firing also, it appeared. The big foreman had pulled up abruptly, listened a moment, then turned in his saddle to beckon his men on still faster. At the moment Bull was leading his men through a narrow arroyo, the walls of which were so sheer that they were almost perpendicular.

Pete had taken some chances and had ridden at full gallop over ground that would have daunted a less reckless rider. But chasing mustangs had given him the skills such riding demanded. So now once again he was in a position to fire down upon Bull as he approached head-on.

Pete was lying prone on a small patch of grass, with boulders crowding close upon him on both sides. Ahead of him was an unobstructed view of the narrow trail that wound through the arroyo. Sighting along the rifle barrel, he caught Bull's chest and head in his sights and tracked the man for a while, his fingers sweating against the wood of the stock. Bull's chest grew larger, steadily larger. Pete held his breath as he picked out the lines of Bull's brutal, heavy face. Lowering the barrel slightly until the sights rested on the ground just in front of his horse's hooves, Pete squeezed the trigger.

The crash of the shot shattered the air. A tiny geyser of dirt and shattered stone erupted in front of Bull's horse. The animal reared. Pete fired again. There was another explosion at the horse's feet. Pete could barely hear the horse's frantic whinny as it tried to climb into the sky.

Bull could no longer control the terrified animal and was thrown out of the saddle. He landed on his back, heavily, and for a moment Pete thought the Jinglebob foreman might have been injured critically, or at least seriously enough to immobilize him. But then he saw Bull push himself to a sitting position and peer dazedly up at the rocks from which Pete's shots had come.

Pete turned his attention then to the other riders rushing up through the arroyo to help their foreman. Levering swiftly, he sent a murderous volley at the rocky ground before them. In a panic, those in front reined up, while those behind began to fall back. With cold deliberation, Pete sent rounds ricocheting off the rock walls just above their heads. He could see the terrified men ducking frantically as they tugged their horses backward, then wheeled them around in the narrow defile and started to gallop back the way they had come.

Leaping to his feet, Pete clambered down the slope. He had left his horse tethered in a clump of bullberry. Mounting up swiftly, he rode down the arroyo, his rifle trained on the dazed foreman. Bull pushed himself upright, his face dark with fury.

"You remember Tim Bronson, my ranch hand?" Pete asked.

"Sure."

"The doc in Harmony had to amputate his hand. I'm bringing you in for aggravated assault. Now unbuckle that gunbelt."

Grudgingly, Bull did as he was told.

"Now come along, you son of a bitch," Pete told him.

"What the hell do you mean?"

"I mean you got a walk ahead of you," Pete said.

"Walk? Where?"

"To Harmony."

168

"You got to be out of your mind. That's better than twenty miles!"

"So it is," said Pete, uncoiling his lariat.

Bull tried to pull back, but the expertly thrown rope settled over his shoulders, and before he could shrug out of it, Pete had yanked the noose shut. Snubbing the rope on his saddle horn, Pete turned his horse about and began to ride.

He heard Bull cry out, and turned to look back. Bull, lying prone on the rocky ground, had both hands extended, his fists clenched about the rope. A deep gash had been opened on his forehead.

"You want me to go slower, Bull?"

Bull scrambled anxiously to his feet. "Yes, for God's sake!"

With a nod, Pete urged his horse on at a walk, then turned down a narrow trail and entered a thick stand of pine.

Before long he and the big foreman were out of sight, and the confused, disorganized riders who rode back up through the arroyo could find no sign to follow on the smooth, sloping trail of pine needles that led back down the mountainside.

After a short conference, they regrouped and continued on through the canyon, heading into the foothills toward the dam. But they no longer rode with the same urgency. They were leaderless and disheartened. A few were for pulling back entirely and returning to the Jinglebob. They kept going, however, but they were no longer the same cohesive unit they had been with Bull Schofield leading them.

* * *

All five powder barrels were now in place. Longarm stood by Nate as the cattleman finished splitting the fuse and took out his tin of matches.

From the trail came a shout. "Longarm! Look down there! It's Dunstrom and his men!"

Longarm glanced down the canyon. Riding full tilt up the dry watercourse came Harmon Dunstrom, his son beside him. As they swept closer, Longarm saw four more Jinglebob riders strung out behind them. They must have heard the shooting and were coming now as fast as they could.

Turning to Nate, Longarm put a restraining hand on his shoulder. "Hold it," he said. "If you light the fuse now, you'll kill those poor stupid bastards down there."

"What in hell would be wrong with that?" Nate growled. But he closed the tin and pocketed it.

"Once they move out of the riverbed, we can blow it," Longarm assured him.

"How do we get them to do that?" Nate asked.

"Fire on them."

Longarm and Nate hurried out from under the dam. With Bingham joining them, they scrambled down the trail until they reached a spot that gave them an unobstructed view of the canyon below. Levering their rifles, they waited for the six riders to come closer.

Watching Harmon sweep closer, Longarm wondered at the arrogance of the man. He must have heard the shooting that had subsided only a few minutes before, and he knew that Nate Simpson and Ben Overmeyer were up here with black powder, or at least were close by. At any moment, therefore, the dam now hanging over his head could blow, sending a mountain of water down upon him. Yet the man continued to ride full tilt up the empty watercourse, evidently supremely confident that the gunfire he heard had been his own guards ending whatever threat Simpson and Overmeyer represented.

"Fire over their heads," Longarm said. "All we want to do is turn them back. As soon as they realize their guards are gone and we have them cold, they'll pull up and go back."

"Are you sure of that?" Nate demanded.

"If they come after us, we can take them," Bingham assured. "Do as Longarm says."

But before either man could fire, a rifle cracked, its sharp, startling report echoing throughout the canyon. Longarm could not be certain, but he thought the shot had come from the pines on the slope high above them. He saw the riders below pull up just as another shot came from the pines.

The echo of this second report, however, was immediately lost in the titanic explosion which followed. The ground shuddered under their feet.

"My God! The dam!" Bingham called.

"Someone's shooting at them kegs of black powder!" said Nate.

The three men looked back. A hole had been blasted from the left side of the dam, and through it a stream of water was spurting. Then a boulder shot from the hole like a cork from a bottle.

Though the dam had been weakened, miraculously, it held.

Longarm glanced back down at Harmon and the other riders. Only now were they beginning to spur their horses for the trail above the watercourse.

But they were too late. Another shot came from the pine-clad slope. This time the bullet slammed into one of the two powder kegs placed together at the center of the dam and the explosion that followed flung Longarm, Nate, and the sheriff violently to the ground. With an awesome roar the dam gave way. Longarm and the other two scrambled quickly to higher ground as the rock ledge beneath them shuddered convulsively.

Glancing back as he clawed his way up the slope, Longarm saw the broken logs bouncing and twisting into the air like enormous tenpins before slamming back into the crushing torrent of water roaring in full cry down the canyon. The sound it made as it scoured its way past the canyon walls was deafening. Even the teeth in Longarm's head ached, it seemed, from the constant buffeting. The universe had gone mad.

And Harmon Dunstrom, his son, and four Jinglebob riders had been swept away in a twinkling.

"Nate," Longarm cried above the roar, "I don't know who the hell fired those shots. But maybe you just better get out of here. Get on back down to that wagon and go!"

Nate nodded. The dam was gone, his mission accomplished. But there was no great triumph, Longarm noted, on the cattleman's face. Hauling his rifle out of the pine needles, Nate started to pick his way back down the slope to his wagon. Earlier, they had brought Ben Overmeyer's body down to the wagon and wrapped him in a tarpaulin. Nate would have the unpleasant solitary task of burying his neighbor and good friend.

Bingham looked at Longarm. "Now what?"

"Let's see if we can find out who it was up there in

those pines who wanted to kill Harmon Dunstrom more than we did."

Bingham nodded grimly.

Longarm started up the steep slope. He had caught sight of a thin wisp of smoke over the tops of the pines a second after the first shot. He was certain now that it had marked the sniper's position. The moment he saw it, he had fixed the location in his memory. Now he climbed steadily toward the spot.

The two men did not have far to go. Jill Dunstrom stepped out from a clump of piñon, her rifle trained on them, her eyes cold and calculating. Bingham pulled up, surprised and astonished. Longarm took a deep breath, remembering an earlier time when a hidden rifle as unerringly accurate as Jill's had cut down Pedro Morales and his woman.

"It was you, then," Longarm said to Jill. "You're the one who shot Pedro and his wife. Why?"

"To save your fool life. Why else?"

"It was more than that."

She shrugged. "Yes, that's true. I did not want that foolish Mexican to tell you I was the one who hired the Warrens to kill Dennis. As soon as I learned you would be going after Pedro, I knew if he were to be threatened with the prospect of a hanging, he would tell why he and the Warrens were holding up the stage."

"He tried to tell us. I realize that now."

Bingham spoke up then. "They were robbing the stage to get their payoff. That was how you made contact with them to pay them for killing your husband."

"Yes. Paid them and continued to pay them. It was getting tiresome, very expensive, and very complicated.

173

Much too complicated. I have to admit, Custis Long, you did me a favor, killing them."

"I assure you that was not my intention. What next, Jill? You've just killed Harmon and Kelsey, making you the sole owner of the Jinglebob. Will that satisfy you?"

She smiled very coldly. "Of course. That is all I have ever wanted. Now drop your guns, both of you."

Carefully, Longarm let his rifle fall to the ground. Beside him, Bingham dropped his rifle also, then unbuckled his gunbelt and let it slip off his hips.

"Longarm," Jill said with a slight smile, "take that Colt of yours out of your cross-draw rig very carefully— and don't forget that nice little derringer, the one I saw taken from you during the holdup."

Reluctantly and very slowly, Longarm reached in and withdrew the .44, then the derringer, and dropped them both to the ground.

"Now turn around, both of you, and go back down the slope. Keep going until you reach the canyon rim."

Longarm and Bingham had both watched Pedro Morales and his woman go down before Jill's ruthless fire. They realized the futility of trying to reason with such a scorpion.

They reached the canyon rim. Below them the waters were still in a turmoil. Logs, tree roots, and debris of all kinds swirled about, caught in backwaters and whirlpools. Though the current had slowed considerably by this time, the water was still sweeping down the channel at a fierce rate.

Jill raised her rifle at Longarm and smiled. Bingham cried out and pushed Longarm down just as Jill fired. The round caught Bingham in the side and sent him staggering back. He lost his footing and, with a cry, disappeared over the canyon rim. On his hands and knees, Longarm saw Bingham tumble headlong into the swift, black waters.

Longarm turned on Jill in a fury. "Go ahead! Fire on me! I'll still take you with me, you damned witch!" he cried, rushing her.

Frantically, she levered a fresh cartridge into her rifle and got off a shot. But the round missed. By then Longarm had reached her. With one powerful swipe of his hand, he knocked the rifle away. Jill spun away from him and started to run. Longarm reached out and managed to grab her arm. She yanked free of him, then raced back down the slope. He snatched up her rifle and fired at the ground before her feet.

She pulled up and turned to face him.

"You can't kill me, Custis," she told him. "You can't shoot a woman in cold blood. Not a woman you've lain with—not a woman you have loved!"

She was smiling when she said that, but the smile froze on her face. Harmon Dunstrom's huge figure materialized from the pines beside her. He was drenched clear to the bone and a deep gash had laid open the left side of his face. Jill cringed back from the towering figure.

"It was you did it!" Harmon cried. "I heard everything!" Longarm could hardly recognize Dunstrom's voice. It sounded like a cry ripped from the throat of a wounded animal. "I knew it! You killed Dennis! And my son!"

Jill turned to run, but Harmon reached out and caught her.

"Hold it right there, Dunstrom!" Longarm ordered.

Dunstrom did not even bother to look in his direction. He swung Jill over his head and flung her out over the brawling stream. Then he turned on Longarm. Longarm fired. The slug smashed a hole in Dunstrom's chest, slamming him backward. Without a cry, he vanished into the swirling waters.

Chapter 10

Billy Vail shook his head and reached out for the shot-glass. "You've got to understand, Longarm," the marshal said, "how hard that is for me to believe."

"You said it yourself, Billy. Maybe you should've spent more time teaching Charlie when to shoot that sixgun of his instead of how."

To that Vail offered no comment. He tossed down the whiskey and looked gloomily about him. But he wasn't seeing the bright fixtures of the Windsor Hotel's saloon, the shifting layers of blue smoke, the pretty women and well-dressed men—or the long, gold-framed mirror behind the bar that had just been installed.

Instead, Longarm realized, Billy Vail was seeing the sprawled body of his nephew, Charlie's sun-blasted skeleton picked almost clean by the vultures.

Vail looked back at Longarm. "You say Bart Bonham saved your life?"

"He pushed me out of the way. The bullet he took was meant for me. I wouldn't be sitting here in Denver City now, talking to you, if Bart Bonham hadn't been the man he was."

"And you believe his version of what happened?" Vail asked.

"I do, yes."

Billy nodded gloomily, then looked more closely at Longarm. The faint workings of a smile creased his florid face. "Well, now, I'm glad he had the gumption to stop that bullet, then. I'd sure would've hated to lose you, Longarm."

"I wouldn't have like it none, either."

Billy sighed and reached for the bottle. "Thing is," Vail continued, "when you spend half a lifetime nursing a grudge, searching for a son of a bitch you know is responsible for something, you hate like hell to let go of it. You know what I mean?"

"I guess maybe I do."

"It's hard. It purely is." Vail leaned back in his chair. "But it don't have to be impossible. And maybe it's about time I did let go of that whole rotten business."

As he spoke, Vail reached into his shirt pocket and took out the yellowed slip of paper he had been carrying. It was that bill of sale he had made his nephew and Bart Bonham sign so long ago. Unfolding it with great care, he laid it down flat on the table, studied it a moment, then abruptly crumpled it and flung it toward a brass cuspidor. Then he grinned at Longarm. "Kitty's waiting for you, ain't she?"

Longarm smiled. "Yes."

"Well, go to her then. Show her the mile-high city. How's her father doing, by the way?"

"Kitty said he's resting comfortably in his room. There's some rooming houses in the hills above this here mile-high city will take Wilkinson in for a reasonable price. I been inquiring. Maybe this clear air will be just the thing for his lungs."

"Maybe," Vail said encouragingly. "I've seen it do miracles."

Longarm got to his feet and hesitated. He hated leaving Billy like this.

Billy grinned up at him and waved him away. "Go on, get out of here! Just don't be late coming in tomorrow!" he said, scowling comically.

Longarm bid Vail good-night, and moved out to the Windsor Hotel's lobby. Kitty was waiting for him in one of the chairs. At his approach, she got to her feet. Her smile was radiant.

He doffed his hat to her and she took his arm. They had spent the afternoon at some exclusive dress shops, and she looked very nice indeed in the dress they had decided on for that night. It had a tight red velvet bodice, and the hip-hugging skirt had ruffles about the ankles. The hat they had selected to go with her outfit was a saucy item direct from Paris.

But as Longarm stepped out into the night with her, he reflected that Kitty Wilkinson had looked just as beautiful in her homemade dress as she did now in one of

179

Denver's most stylish creations.

"I know just the restaurant," he told her.

She rested her head on his shoulder. "I thought you might. And then what?"

"We'll find something to do, I'm sure."

She hugged his arm. "Yes," she said, her voice husky, "I'm sure we will."

Watch for

LONGARM AND THE CATTLE BARON

sixty-fourth novel in the bold
LONGARM series from Jove

coming in April!